Bishop

TED WOODS

Beaten Track
www.beatentrackpublishing.com

Bishop

First published 2020 by Beaten Track Publishing
Copyright © 2020 Ted Woods

ISBN: 978 1 78645 456 0

Beaten Track Publishing,
Burscough, Lancashire.
www.beatentrackpublishing.com

For my wife Anne, with love and thanks
for her encouragement and occasional suggestions!

Thanks also to Debbie McGowan of Beaten Track
for her help and advice.

Chapter 1

B LOODY BISHOP!" THE words slipped involuntarily from the lips of Canon Anthony Parker, Rector of St. Aidan's, as he sipped his cranberry juice. He usually had breakfast alone as his wife, Annabel, was never an early riser. He had his iPad beside him and had just opened the website of Daneford Diocese in which he served.

There, under 'Latest News', he read that the bishop had appointed a new archdeacon. It wasn't Anthony, but a relative newcomer to the diocese, imported from the Church of England by the bishop as a fellow evangelical with a 'Church Growth and Fresh Expression' brief—the current fad in Church circles. And to make matters worse, the new archdeacon, Guy Morgan, was Anthony's next-door neighbour, parochially speaking.

***

"'Bloody Bishop!" The words were said with feeling as Susan Shilling opened a letter bearing the episcopal crest of Daneford Diocese. Indeed, the oversized crest, along with the bishop's details, covered half of the page of the letter inside.

> Dear Susan,
>
> I regret that you were not recommended for training for the ordained ministry by the selectors at the recent Selection Conference. I know how disappointed...

Susan's Diocesan Director of Ordinands had been enthusiastic in encouraging her to go forward for selection, and so had those in whom she had confided about her burgeoning vocation. But her interview with the diocesan bishop before the Conference had not gone well. For some reason, he had been decidedly cool and unsupportive. Was it because she had been a member of the cathedral congregation and not a card-carrying evangelical? The bishop had been at the Conference as a selector, but, of course, had not interviewed her then. However, that wouldn't have stopped him from putting a spanner in the works when the selectors came together to discuss the candidates. She had a sneaking suspicion that was what had happened.

**

"Bloody Bishop!" The words hissed out of the mouth of Harry White as he put down the phone. Harry was one of the parochial nominators in St. Columba's in Daneford Diocese and was their link man with the bishop in the slow-moving process of appointing a new rector.

The four parochial nominators had been unanimous in their choice from early on in the vacancy. They had done their homework, and, in fact, had taken the initiative and approached a promising young rector, Steve Adams, in the next-door diocese. They had made their views and reasons known at the first meeting of the Board of Nomination. But the bishop kept suggesting that they should consider other possible candidates, none of whom—they knew—were suitable or would fit into the slightly High Church style of St. Columba's. It might become a showdown, but they were sticking to their guns in advance of a second meeting of the Board. But the bishop had phoned Harry to tell him that a decision would have to be deferred as he, the bishop, had just received an updated report from the Diocesan Architect stipulating that further work had to be carried out on the St. Columba's Rectory before it could be passed as suitable for a new rector and their family.

Harry knew, just as the bishop knew, that once three months had elapsed since the calling of the first Board of Nomination and no appointment had been made, the appointment technically fell to the bishop to make.

The 'bloody bishop', about to get his own way again, was Arthur Easterby, or, to give him his full title, The Right Reverend Arthur Ronald Stephen Easterby, Bishop of Daneford.

Chapter 2

AMBITION IS NOT uncommon in clergy, and, it's true to say, most theological students harbour thoughts of becoming a bishop. Indeed, after ordination, some continue to nurse that ambition as they seek to climb the greasy pole of preferment.

Being a bishop was an ambition that was never far from the mind of Arthur Easterby, both before and after ordination.

The 'son of a rectory'—his father was the archdeacon of a rural diocese—Arthur had never known a time when he hadn't wanted to be a clergyman. True, he had toyed with the idea of being a racing driver or a pilot, and later, a pop star, but these were the dreams of all young boys. He always came back to the reality of wanting to be ordained. On leaving school, he had attended—and been recommended for—training for ordination by the Church of Ireland Selection Conference.

Academically clever, he had gone to read theology at an English university, graduating with an honours degree, planning to return to Ireland and train for ministry in the Church of Ireland's Theological Institute in Dublin. Because he already had a theology degree, he was allowed to study for a Master's at the Irish School of Ecumenics whilst attending some lectures at the Institute.

Able, articulate, confident and brimming with evangelical certainty—not to mention three Christian names—Arthur was tipped by staff in the Theological Institute to end up with a purple shirt sooner or later.

"What do you make of Arthur Easterby?" a new student asked of the others as they met in the local pub after Compline.

"You mean 'ARSE'?" laughed one of the second-years. Seeing the puzzled face of the new boy, he went on to explain, "Arthur Ronald Stephen Easterby—A.R.S.E! How could his mother and father have missed that?!"

"But he never seems to join us for a drink," complained another new student.

"That's because he's not doing the same course as the rest of us," explained the second-year student. "He already has a theology degree, so he's doing a Master's in the School of Ecumenics and only has to attend some of our lectures. Seemingly, or so he says, there are all sorts of seminars in the evening that he has to attend. As St. Paul might have put it, 'Arthur is *in* the Institute but not *of* it'!"

And that gave Arthur a huge amount of freedom away from the prying eyes of staff and fellow students. Arthur had a thing for the girls and they for him, and not all of his evenings were taken up with theological seminars.

He had one very narrow escape.

At a seminar on community relations in the city, his eye rested on a very attractive girl who was helping with refreshments, and he went over to talk to her. He was taken with her and she with him. She was from the country and was working in an office in Dublin. Both for something to do in the evening, and also to supplement her salary so she could afford a flat for just herself, she helped with refreshments at the School of Ecumenics.

She, too, was good-looking with a good figure, and she was easy to talk to. Arthur and she started dating, and soon he ended up in her flat after evenings out. He was always able to give some plausible excuse for his late returns to the Institute.

Then came the bombshell. She was pregnant! As a previous principal of the (then) Theological College once remarked, "The lower the church, the hotter the court!"

What were they to do? What was Arthur going to do? She wanted Arthur to marry her quietly in a few months' time and seek permission to move into her flat as husband and wife. She could continue working while he finished his studies, and then they could all move together for his first curacy, QED.

But that wasn't on Arthur's radar. What would people think? What would they say? It would probably be forgotten in time, but more immediately—in his mind—it would affect his standing and reputation among rectors and bishops. In a church as small as the Church of Ireland, news like that travelled widely and lost nothing in the telling.

There was no doubt that the child to be born was his, but love and loyalty, not to mention responsibility, went out the door as Arthur dropped his girlfriend like a hot brick and disappeared off the scene. She was too kind and decent to pursue him and make an issue of it.

She had their baby, and Arthur never bothered to find out how she was or whether the child was a boy or a girl. Maintenance for mother and child never entered his head. He left her to fend for herself.

Arthur Ronald Stephen Easterby truly was an arse.

Chapter 3

No one ever got to hear about Arthur's secret, nor of his shameful behaviour.

Coming up to the 'curacy round', when rectors appointing curates received the CVs of final-year students, and potential ordinands got the profiles of parishes looking for a curate, Arthur was the first choice of many rectors hoping to appoint a curate.

Arthur had prioritised which parishes he would like. Not only did they need to be 'plum' parishes in affluent areas, but he needed to get out of Dublin, just in case he came across his erstwhile former girlfriend and his child.

As first choice, he put down a large suburban parish in a well-to-do area in the eastern suburbs of Belfast. The rector was also the archdeacon, so, he reasoned, if he played his cards right and did a good job, he could get recommended for a good parish after the curacy and not have to go to some small rural backwater in the middle of nowhere for his first incumbency.

He was appointed to the parish of his first choice. He did a good job as curate and kept his nose clean. The archdeacon's confidence in him grew, and soon he was quite happy to leave Arthur in charge of the parish and even chair the Select Vestry when, as archdeacon, he had to be elsewhere on diocesan business.

Arthur was a frequent guest in the rectory, and not just for staff meetings on a Tuesday morning.

The archdeacon's wife, Daisy, took a great shine to Arthur, and he often dropped in on her at various times during the week for a cup of coffee and a bit of parish gossip.

Daisy and the archdeacon had married later in life and had an only child: a daughter named Sarah, who was in her final year of university where she was studying law. She lived at home and commuted daily to lectures, so she was around the rectory quite a bit. She sang in the choir and was a leader of the Sunday night youth fellowship, which was also one of Arthur's responsibilities as a curate.

Daisy was not the only mother in the parish who had an eligible daughter and who harboured hopes of Arthur as a future son-in-law. He received frequent invitations to Sunday lunch as mothers and daughters in the parish hoped that the way to a single curate's heart might be through his stomach. Those same mothers kept him supplied with cooked meals and apple tarts and cakes, which they left on his doorstep, along, of course, with a wee note to say who they were from. His freezer was overflowing with their offerings.

But Arthur knew he had to keep in with Daisy and the archdeacon. He would never be forgiven if he took up with any other girl in the parish, and a parish in the back end of nowhere would become a reality. Plus, Sarah was pretty and intelligent, and, he thought, would make a suitable bishop's wife eventually. Arthur already had his career path mapped out.

He had learned from past mistakes. While their kissing and cuddling was passionate and full-blooded, he kept himself in check and made sure their relationship remained chaste. He had escaped once, and there would be no anonymity or second chance in the fish bowl of parish life.

Sarah and Arthur were married two and a half years later on a beautiful, sunny April day. The church was packed with guests and gawkers. The bishop conducted the service as Sarah was proudly walked up the aisle on the arm of her father.

Everything was magnificent—the outfits, the flowers, the music, even the weather—and the couple themselves looked stunning: Arthur, tall and handsome; Sarah, beautiful and radiant. Marquees had been erected on the rectory lawn for the reception. Everything went without a hitch, and the next day, the happy couple set off for their honeymoon in Barbados.

They weren't long home when a pleasant suburban parish in the diocese became vacant. With the archdeacon's influence, Arthur was appointed as rector, and he and Sarah moved into the newly refurbished rectory beside the church. As usual in such situations, the glebe wardens had been reluctant to do much work, but the archdeacon's voice had prevailed.

In his first parish, as in his curacy, Arthur succeeded and was well liked. Two children—a boy, Crispin, and a girl, Diana—were born in quick succession. The parishioners were delighted; they always loved to see young children in the rectory. However, Sarah was not as impressed and insisted that Arthur have 'the snip'. She wanted to get back to her career as soon as possible.

As a clergyman, Arthur was a good preacher and a good chairman of committees. He made friends easily, especially with those who mattered. The numbers attending services began to increase. His predecessor, luckily for Arthur, had been a bit of a disaster in running the parish, so everything Arthur did was noted and approved of. He was also beginning to get noticed in the diocese, and his reputation was enhanced. Soon he was elected onto various diocesan committees and even to General Synod.

It wasn't hard to get elected onto General Synod in small rural dioceses; it was much more difficult in the populous dioceses of Northern Ireland. Needless to say, in the competitive clergy scene, his election was not popular with some of the older clergy who had been waiting many years for their turn.

Five years later, Sarah's father, the archdeacon, decided to retire, and it was no surprise to the cynics among the clergy, of which there were many, when Arthur was appointed to his father-in-law's parish. Not that the retired archdeacon had anything to do with the appointment... Of course not! He only gave his opinion, whether he was asked or not.

"Well, it won't be long until Arse is also made an archdeacon," the cynics mused. And they were right. Arthur became one of the youngest canons in the history of the diocese. A few years later, he was appointed by the bishop to represent the diocese as a canon of the national cathedral, St. Patrick's in Dublin, and a few years after that, at the tender age of forty-five, he was made archdeacon.

It was an enviable upward career trajectory which would surely continue on its path to the episcopacy and the bench of bishops.

Chapter 4

W E NEED SOMEONE young with new ideas to connect with a younger generation," was the general opinion of the local episcopal electors as they met together after the Rt. Revd. Bill Grace announced his retirement from the see of Daneford.

The rumour and speculation mills were already in top gear, both inside and outside the diocese. Bishop-tipping is a national sport in the Church of Ireland—one race-going cleric even produced a runners' card, complete with thinly disguised and uncomplimentary names for the supposed candidates and offering odds. Arthur was listed as 'Rear End'!

Bill Grace had been popular with everyone in the diocese. He was slightly smaller than medium height and had an ample girth which gave him a cuddly look. His grey hair and bushy eyebrows were grandfatherly, he had a great sense of humour, and there always seemed to be a twinkle in his eyes. He remembered people's names, and that endeared him to them.

There was nothing stuffy or pompous about him, and he had a wonderful knack of fitting in with each occasion. He was as happy at a 'low' service as at a liturgical extravaganza in the cathedral.

His one big failing was that he disliked making unpopular decisions. And he was no administrator. In difficult situations, his clergy were never sure whether he was totally behind them, and he had a habit of agreeing with the last person who had spoken with him. One or two clergy had thought he would support them in difficult parish situations, only to find that he had also agreed with those who had complained about them, and this had led to feelings of hurt and uncertainty.

The Daneford episcopal electors met informally to discuss the vacancy and who might be approached to fill it.

"We want a bishop who will look after his or her clergy, who will be a *pastor pastorum*," offered one of the clergy members. "Someone who will support and back up those on the frontline of parish ministry."

"And someone who will be able to comment on social issues and be respected by the press," added a prominent layperson.

And so the meeting went on, suggesting criteria which in the end not even the archangel Gabriel would have met.

"We need to be united behind one candidate," said one of the experienced electors. "If we are divided, so too will be the reps from the other dioceses, leading to a split vote. Then it will pass to the House of Bishops to make the appointment, and goodness knows who we'll get then. So, let's hear of any names you think might be suitable."

The one name that kept coming up was Arthur's.

"He's already an archdeacon and knows how a diocese runs."

"He's done a bloody good job in all the parishes in which he has served."

"I've been on central committees with him, and he always makes sound contributions."

"Yes, and his speeches at General Synod are always worth listening to."

"He's a safe pair of hands."

"And, he's only fifty-four."

Some episcopal electoral meetings, or 'colleges' as they are called, turn out to be bruising and hurtful occasions, but the electoral college for the diocese of Daneford was a model of peace and unity of spirit. Arthur was unanimously proposed by the Daneford electors, and while a member from another diocese proposed another name, there was really no contest; Arthur got well over the two-thirds of the votes needed and was elected on the first count.

***

Arthur, who knew his name was going to be proposed and had cleared his diary for the afternoon, was sitting in his study, not able to concentrate on anything, when the Archbishop of Armagh who chaired the meeting rang to give him the news and to ask if he would accept the nomination.

"Oh, goodness, that was unexpected," he lied. "Sarah's out at work, but let me give her a quick ring and I will be back to you in a few minutes."

Sarah was expecting a call from Arthur. They had endlessly discussed the possibility of Arthur being elected, and his call to her was a formality. Daneford was just outside Dublin where, with her legal contacts, she would be able to further her own career in one of the many companies operating in the capital.

Waiting an extra minute for decency's sake, Arthur returned the archbishop's call and confirmed his acceptance.

"Of course, it will now have to be agreed by the House of Bishops, but I can't foresee any problem there. So, congratulations, the announcement will be made later this afternoon."

Chapter 5

THE THREE MONTHS following Arthur's election were extremely busy. There was a big send-off from his old parish. He had been there for over eleven years and had become well established and well liked, at least by most. In parish life, you can't please all the people all the time, and as always, there was a small group of begrudgers and critics.

But Arthur had no worries about the new curate he had appointed. David McCrea was a man in middle age who had previously worked in a bank. When he had been made redundant as a result of a merger, David's sense of vocation, which had lain dormant for many years, reignited and set him on the path of ordination. No, Arthur was confident that his curate would manage the parish and keep things going until a successor was appointed. And, equally importantly, Arthur was sure that David McCrea wouldn't start changing things in the parish during the vacancy. Anyway, it wasn't his problem now. He had bigger fish to fry.

There were endless meetings and arguments over the refurbishment of the See House. How he wished his father-in-law had still been on some of those committees! He was sent on a 'Baby Bishops' course in England. Then there were consultations with the Dean of Christ Church Cathedral and the Archbishop of Dublin about the order of service for his consecration. What hymns did he want? Who was to preach? What about readers? Daneford Diocesan Office wanted a list of those to be invited as soon as possible. And then there was his installation or 'enthronement' in Daneford Cathedral. More meetings, more minutiae!

Arthur and Sarah moved into the See House ten days before his consecration as bishop. They were both exhausted. The unpacking of endless boxes was taking longer than they thought and taking its toll on their energy levels and tempers.

"That'll do for now," said Sarah, her face etched with tiredness. "I'll have to go for lie down. You can finish unpacking your books."

Arthur went into his spacious study. No energy for unpacking books, he wandered over to the cupboard where his new robes hung. He had bought purple cassocks, a black and a red chimere and a couple of rochets. He had been tempted to order the cope and mitre one or two of his fellow bishops had begun wearing, but that, he felt, might be interpreted as a betrayal of his evangelicalism. For some in that camp, even coloured stoles were still a step too far.

Better try them on—again—just to be sure!

He had ordered purple shirts in a variety of hues, plus a few black shirts. It was becoming fashionable for bishops to wear black occasionally. It sort of showed that they really hadn't got above themselves. Bishops now used their Christian names, always, of course, preceded by the title 'Bishop'. It was pally, yet authoritative, and fooled none of the clergy.

Arthur supposed he would wear the red chimere for his consecration. Although some (pedants) held that a red chimere was an academic gown denoting a doctorate, others argued that in the modern Church it had just become an episcopal garment and so was proper to wear with or without a doctorate. Anyway, Arthur reasoned, as they said in *Fiddler on the Roof,* 'it's tradition!'

Yes, he reflected on his image in the mirror; he did look episcopal. He tried on his episcopal ring, presented by his last diocese, and also a couple of pectoral crosses. One was made from olive wood from Bethlehem. Again, it looked humble and would do for everyday occasions. His in-laws had given him a silver cross whilst Sarah had given him a present of a rather beautiful gold cross with an amethyst in the centre. He would wear the silver one on more formal occasions. The gold one he would wear for services.

There, all sorted. He smiled rather smugly and proudly at himself in the mirror. After the consecration service was over, he would get down to work and sort out Daneford diocese. Top of the list would be the appointment of a new rector to fill St. Stephen's, one of the largest parishes in Daneford which had fallen vacant during the interregnum. And Arthur knew exactly whom he would like to appoint.

Chapter 6

Guy Morgan was the vicar of a large market-town parish in the Midlands of England. Arthur and he had met, and become friends, at various conferences on Church Growth that both had attended, and in Arthur's eyes, Guy had an impressive track record. Over the years, Guy's parish had been transformed from being a poorly attended traditional parish to a thriving, busy, modern church with café services, house groups, pub groups and so on. Evening services had been replaced by a multimedia experience with worship bands, screens and flashing lights. There were Men's Breakfasts, Ladies' Lunches, Kids' Klubs—in fact, something for every age—as well as a very well-run and well-supported food bank.

St. Stephen's in Daneford Diocese was full of potential. The previous rector had had the church roof repaired and renovated the halls but hadn't had the time, nor the energy, to revitalise the spiritual life of the parish. But, in Arthur's opinion, Guy would be just the person to bring life to St. Stephen's and to put Daneford on the map as a diocese 'Going For Growth'. It would do no harm to Arthur's reputation as a new go-ahead bishop in tune with the latest ecclesiastical fixation.

Having set everything up and trained leaders for the various activities, or 'ministries' as he called them, Guy was looking for another challenge.

One of the gifts of the Spirit imparted to bishops when they are consecrated is the ability to talk up the parishes in their dioceses, and when they are looking for someone to come to one of their parishes, they are as good as any estate agent with all their talk about 'challenge' and 'potential'.

Stipends and expenses are also higher in the Church of Ireland than in their sister church in England, and Arthur had persuaded the vestry of St. Stephen's to pay their new rector's utilities. So, all in all, he had a very attractive package to offer Guy Morgan, along with the promise of his wholehearted support, if he could get the Board of Nomination to agree. His fall-back strategy was that if no appointment was made within three months, the appointment became his to make.

The appointment of a new rector for St. Stephen's was Arthur's first experience of chairing a Board of Nomination, and for the representatives of St. Stephen's, it was their first meeting with Arthur as their new bishop. They were on their best behaviour, Arthur was at his friendly and persuasive best, and in that sweetest of honeymoon periods, they agreed on Guy, who, much to Arthur's relief and joy, accepted the nomination.

***

Guy hit St. Stephen's like a storm. He erected a screen at the front of the church (to save paper!), updated the sound system so there was now a large mixer desk at the back of the church—a must for lively evangelical churches. Chairs replaced pews and, of course, there was a drum kit in the sanctuary. Banners hung around the walls, and Guy had the back quarter of the large church converted into two floors. On the ground floor was a spacious entrance area fitted out with a coffee bar for refreshments on one side, with a soundproofed children's play area on the other. On the second floor, the 'mezzanine floor', there was a large meeting room and two smaller offices for the rector and parish secretary, or 'PA', as Guy liked to call her.

It was an ambitious and imaginative project, though not everyone went along with it, or the small fortune it cost, and left St. Stephen's. Others left because they didn't find Guy's full-on evangelistic approach to their liking, or the fact that he seldom wore robes. Some found refuge in the next-door parish of St. Aidan's whose rector was Canon Anthony Parker. St. Aidan's was a more traditional, middle-of-the-road church where everything was done 'decently and in order'.

But Guy didn't seem to mind. In fact, he hardly seemed to notice. The loss of a few fuddy-duddies was more than offset by the influx of young singles and young families—the very ones Guy was setting out to attract. St. Stephen's was becoming the 'in' church, and Guy's reputation was growing.

Chapter 7

THE FIRST TWO years of Arthur's episcopate seemed to go by in a flurry of meetings, services and getting to know the parishes and people of Daneford. There were clergy on the move, retirements, and parishes to fill. His archdeacon was among the retirements, but this was not a cause for worry. In fact, Arthur was very pleased because since getting Guy Morgan to St. Stephen's, he had decided that when the post of archdeacon became vacant, he would offer the position to Guy. It had come about sooner than he'd expected, but now he and Guy could really put Daneford on the ecclesiastical map.

On top of all the diocesan duties there were also central Church responsibilities. In the Church of Ireland, it seemed that no central Church committee could meet without a bishop being present, preferably in the chair, and he had been allocated his share of committees. Then there were separate meetings and retreats for bishops. It was all go!

Sarah got a position with a large legal firm in Dublin and had thrown herself into the work. It all meant that she and Arthur had little time to themselves and really only caught up with each other as they drove to functions that required the presence of the bishop's wife.

Arthur was not complaining; he relished the workload and liked to be thought of as a busy man. He also prided himself as being a decisive and business-like leader, the very opposite to his predecessor, old Bill Grace.

Among aspects of his role that he had to come to grips with was being patron of all the Church of Ireland schools in Daneford Diocese, and this meant signing off on appointments, making sure schools were compliant with legislation, procedures and protocols (which seemed to be ever-changing) and dealing with problems that inevitably arose.

Arthur tried to visit as many schools as possible and get to know the principals, who were usually very clued in about educational matters. To many of the local clergy, having to chair the board of management or just be a member of the board was another, often unwelcome, layer to their already complicated lives and they weren't always as up to date as the principals.

One Monday morning, he visited St. Olaf's National School in Lislea, one of Daneford's thriving market towns. He was due to speak at assembly and then have a cup of coffee with the local rector, Revd. Wendy Morris, and the principal, Laurence Finch.

Laurence ran a tight ship, and Arthur sensed he was a man on top of his job and his staff. While Laurence's relationship with Wendy was cordial enough, Arthur detected a slight apprehensiveness on Wendy's part, as though she had to tread warily around Laurence.

The assembly went on longer than usual: it wasn't every week that they had a bishop, and various classes did special presentations of Bible stories or read poems they had written. The school choir sang some of their pieces. Then Laurence gave Arthur a conducted tour of the school, which had recently been extended and renovated and of which he was immensely proud. By the time they were done and ready for coffee, Wendy had to dash off to take a funeral.

But Arthur was in no hurry that morning; he found Laurence to be knowledgeable and informative about educational matters. Here was someone, Arthur felt, whom he could consult about some of the school matters that crossed his desk. Laurence was also on the Diocesan Board of Education, and he could be a useful ally if and when contentious matters arose.

So they had a second cup of coffee. Laurence was a member of St. Olaf's parish, and while he did not criticise Wendy as the rector, he certainly gave the impression she was not as easy to get on with as her predecessor had been. Laurence waxed lyrical about old Canon Watson, how cooperative he had always been in school matters and how he had been universally liked in the parish. Arthur noted the subtext and filed it away in his mind, but he was mightily impressed with Laurence Finch and the way he ran St. Olaf's school.

"Oh my, how the time has flown," said Arthur, looking at his watch when Laurence offered a *third* cup of coffee. "I really mustn't keep you any longer from your duties."

With a quick, cordial shake of the hand, Arthur was off, back to the See House for his meeting with Guy Morgan— the incoming Archdeacon of Daneford.

Chapter 8

DANEFORD DIOCESAN COUNCIL met the week Guy's appointment was announced. Canon Anthony Parker, rector of St. Aidan's, entered the boardroom and looked for a place to sit.

"I'm going to have to change my seat," he muttered to himself on the way in. He usually sat at the far end of the large boardroom table, directly opposite the bishop's place as chairman. But now he had been passed over for promotion, he could no longer bear to look at him every time he lifted his head from his papers. He found a vacant chair along the left-hand side of the long table and ignored the mumblings of those already seated, aware his actions were almost unheard of in Church meetings. People had *their* seats, and woe to any newcomer who sat in the wrong place. Anthony didn't care whose seat it was.

A few of the older members came over to commiserate with him before the meeting started, insensitively telling him that they had been sure he would have been the next archdeacon as he had all the necessary experience. He knew they meant well, so he smiled, spread his hands in a self-deprecating manner, tilted his head modestly and said, "Oh, well..." but he was beginning to get irritated by their remarks.

The room filled up. The bishop and his new archdeacon entered and took their seats. Only then did Anthony realise that in his new seat he now had a clear view of the new archdeacon who sat on the bishop's right!

Anthony was disgusted that the Ven. Guy Morgan wasn't dressed as an archdeacon should be. He didn't even wear a jacket but a rather garish jumper over his light-blue clerical shirt. Anthony disapproved of younger clergy wearing jeans and sweaters with their clerical shirts. But an archdeacon dressing like that as well? It was an outrage!

Arthur opened with prayer and then welcomed the new archdeacon. "As you will no doubt have read on the diocesan website, I have appointed the Reverend Guy Morgan to be my new archdeacon. I have known Guy for a great number of years and admired his ministry in many parts of England where he has been at the forefront of the Growth and Renewal Agenda and been instrumental in planting some new Fresh Expressions of Church. His ministry over the water is well-known, and he has been an inspirational speaker at many Church Growth conferences. It was a particular joy to me that he agreed to come to Daneford two years ago, and we have all seen the fruits of his labours in revitalising St. Stephen's. I can now confidently announce to you that Going For Growth is to be the new motto for Daneford Diocese as we seek the help of the Holy Spirit—and our new archdeacon—to be a bigger church in Daneford."

Guy replied that he was looking forward to his new role and that he would soon be arranging individual meetings with all the clergy of Daneford to initiate a programme of MDR—Ministerial Development Review—which was part of Church life in England. He was also keen to talk to clergy about how their parishes might grow and initiate new missional activities and perhaps, even plant new churches.

Anthony watched the shutters come down on a few tired clerical eyes. Like him, they had been through the Decade of

Evangelism, Church 21 initiatives, Parish Audits—every latest fad—and now, *Going for Growth*.

"Dear God," he said to the cleric next to him, "When will they ever learn? Don't they realise that good liturgy, good preaching and good pastoral care is all that is needed?"

They would be inundated with more forms to fill in, more statistics to be returned, more seminars to attend—and more money to raise.

"Wouldn't it be nice if bishops and archdeacons left the clergy to get on with the job we were trained for?" whispered the cleric in reply. "And maybe even visit them once in a while, just to show they care."

That would have been Anthony's priority if he had been made archdeacon. In his thirty-five years of ministry, he had only had two pastoral visits from his bishop, and one from an archdeacon. The first episcopal visit had been during his second curacy, when he had been put in charge of a large new housing estate with many social problems. It had been hard going, but the bishop and the archdeacon had called one morning to 'walk in his moccasins', as the bishop had put it, and to see how he and his young wife were faring.

Anthony had been tremendously grateful. Before leaving his house, the bishop had mentioned that if he and his wife ever ran short of money for essentials, the diocese had a discretionary fund which could help out. Anthony hadn't needed to call on the fund, but he appreciated the offer. More than that, he felt appreciated.

His other episcopal visit was when he was in a rural parish and the bishop's car had broken down one night in the vicinity of his rectory. The bishop phoned Anthony and had stayed the night in the rectory. Anthony had got the car fixed the next morning and sent the bishop on his way after lunch. But it had hardly been a pastoral visit. In fact, Anthony had given pastoral care to the bishop!

"Agreed," Anthony murmured back to his neighbour. "They're all managers now and have forgotten how to be pastors pastorum."

Arthur glared at the two whispering clergy, but Anthony, for one, didn't care how rude it might look.

Chapter 9

SUSAN SHILLING POURED herself another cup of coffee and looked again at the letter she had received from the Bishop of Daneford telling her that she had not been recommended for ordination. "'I know how disappointed you must feel...' *Disappointed*!" She sniffed. Devastated would have been nearer the mark.

Susan was thirty-five years old, single and taught in a large primary school in Lislea, one of Daneford's market towns. Originally from a rural village, she had moved to Lislea after training college. Now a permanent teacher in St. Olaf's School, she was able to afford a mortgage and was buying her own house. She enjoyed teaching and had felt fulfilled, but situations had developed recently that prompted her to consider changing her career.

First, she had started attending Daneford Cathedral about five miles from Lislea. She didn't want to attend St. Olaf's, the church to which the school was connected. It would mean being accosted by anxious parents before and after services. She would probably be asked to help with children's activities, which might compromise her role and authority as a teacher, and anyway, she liked the traditional liturgy and the good music of the cathedral. She could be anonymous there, and had joined the Cathedral Study Group, appreciating the explorative rather than dogmatic way topics were discussed.

As her faith was stretched, it grew deeper, and she felt the stirrings of a vocation to ordination. In this, she was encouraged by one of the canons who led the study group. Her own rector back home had hinted that she might consider being ordained, and it had stuck in the back of her mind; now it was coming to the foreground of her thoughts.

Secondly, her school had, of late, become an unhappy place. Her principal, Laurence Finch, liked to get his own way—all the time. He had a rather abrasive manner when dealing with parents, especially those who had complaints of any kind, not least about their child's progress. Schools, particularly in suburbia, were increasingly seen by parents as service providers, and although parents were asked for 'voluntary' contributions towards the running of the school, most regarded it as a fee. So if they were not happy, they, as customers, complained.

In the good old days when Laurence began teaching, parents automatically took the side of the teacher over their children, but that attitude was no longer guaranteed in today's consumer society. In fact, more often the opposite was the case, and Laurence Finch didn't like himself or his teachers being challenged. In fact, he was known to phone the more timid parents after a meeting and tell them what he thought of them. Yet to the well-off and the influential, and those who might be able to do the school a favour or provide them with free or cut-price equipment, he was as obsequious as an undertaker.

He ran a tight ship and liked the minimum of disruption and interference.

Susan called to mind the way Laurence had dealt with the Stone family. Jason and Joy Stone had moved into the parish with their two children, Jake and Joshua, after Jason was promoted with the bank. Jake was eight and Joshua was five, and the family were regular church attenders. When they applied to St. Olaf's school for their boys, they were asked to provide a note from the rector to confirm they were parishioners, and the Revd. Wendy Morris was more than happy to provide it and fully support their application.

It should all have been straightforward. But Laurence Finch contacted the Stones' previous school and discovered that Jake had ADHD and could be quite disruptive in class.

First, Laurence tried to make a case saying there was no room in third class for Jake; the only space, he said, was in Senior Infants for Joshua. But, he told the parents, he was sure they would prefer that their children both attend the same school and suggested the Stones try elsewhere.

The Revd. Wendy Morris was chair of the school's board of management, and when the Stones told her of Laurence's decision, she arranged a meeting with the principal, armed with the board's admission criteria document, which clearly stated all parishioners of St. Olaf's were to be offered a place, and as the Stones were parishioners...

Laurence Finch blustered on about the size of the class and having a disruptive pupil in it, but Wendy was having none of it and stood her ground. Jake and Joshua had to be admitted. If not, she said, she would bring it to the board of management.

It was directly after that meeting that Susan had knocked on Laurence's office door.

She and Joy had grown up in the same village and had attended the same primary school. Thus, when Joy discovered Susan was a teacher at St. Olaf's, she made contact with her and asked how she might go about trying to reverse the principal's decision. Of course Susan had promised she would put in a good word from them with Laurence Finch, but what a day she picked!

He accused her of trying to undermine his authority as principal. He told her that she was being disloyal and didn't have the school's best interest at heart—"Has Wendy Morris put you up to this?" he demanded. Were the two of them collaborating against him? The tirade went on for fifteen minutes, and Susan retreated from his office ashen-faced and shaking.

Just a year previously, when Susan's mother had died, Laurence couldn't have been more helpful, even organising a hamper of food from the school to be delivered to Susan on her return from the funeral.

That was what he was like. He bought loyalty, and when he was crossed, his fury and vindictiveness knew no bounds.

***

After Susan left his office, Laurence turned to his computer and sent an aggrieved email to the Bishop of Daneford, who was the school patron, accusing both Susan Shilling and Wendy Morris of conspiring to undermine his authority as principal. Reluctantly, and with bad grace, he signed off by saying he would find room for both boys.

***

Arthur soaked up information and retained it. No wonder, then, that Susan had received such a frosty reception when Arthur interviewed her before going to Selection Conference.

Chapter 10

Harry White was very much the 'elder lemon' of St. Saviour's parish. An engineer by profession, he had, up to a few years previously, run his own building business specialising in old buildings, including churches. He had often been employed by local parishes when work had to be done on churches, halls or rectories. He'd also been used by the diocese and, indeed, by the wider Church in doing surveys and assessments. Now retired, he had handed the business over to his son, also an engineer.

Harry had many Church contacts both through his professional work and through his involvement in diocesan and central committees, and was a well-known and respected figure in Church circles.

When it came to matters relating to St. Saviour's, his voice and opinion were always listened to, and they generally carried the day. If the rector of St. Saviour's wanted anything done, he went to Harry first and made sure he got him onside.

Harry was a glebe warden, a member of the parish finance committee and a parochial nominator. With regard to the latter, he kept his ears open when clergy were being discussed. Harry, of course, had been the first to know of Canon McKeever's impending retirement from St. Saviour's after thirty years at the helm. He also knew that the parish badly needed somebody with fresh thinking and a new approach.

Denis McKeever, though universally loved, had become ministerially stale and hadn't moved with the times. Services which were acceptable to congregations twenty years ago now just seemed to lack imagination, and while older members of the congregation liked them, the younger families were just not staying. Instead they went to neighbouring parishes where younger clergy were more family focused and where there were midweek activities for children.

St. Saviour's was haemorrhaging young families, and Harry White and his fellow nominators knew that the person they chose as Denis McKeever's successor was vital for the future of the parish.

Harry had heard good reports of a young clergyman, Steve Adams, who had taken on a similar situation in a neighbouring diocese. Steve Adams had revitalised St. Patrick's, introducing clubs for kids, setting up study groups and modernising the liturgy, and was assiduous in pastoral care. St. Patrick's had once been known as 'The Fridge' for its lack of friendliness but was now known for its welcome and inclusiveness. Steve Adams had been in the parish eight years and, in Harry's experience, was probably at the stage of deciding whether to put down roots for the long haul or look for a further challenge.

As St. Saviour's was a bigger parish with the possibility of a curate, Harry felt Steve Adams might be persuaded to think of a move.

Steve was not an out-and-out evangelical but was solidly middle-of-the-road. Nevertheless, he felt that to be moderate was not to be boring. Steve felt passionately that moderation in theology was an exciting and challenging place to be, between prescriptive fundamentalism on the one hand and permissive liberalism on the other. Increasingly in the Church, the middle ground was being squeezed by those who on either side shouted louder.

***

The problem for Steve and other moderates was that questions about innovations such as Fresh Expressions and Growth strategies were often misinterpreted negatively by those who espoused such causes and were not seen simply as an evaluation and exploration of the principles behind such ventures. Steve had asked such questions from the floor at General Synod, and Arthur, perched on the episcopal platform with his fellow bishops, had taken note of what he regarded as criticisms of Growth and Renewal programmes and mentally filed Steve Adams as one he would not have in his diocese.

Harry White had retired from business before Arthur Easterby had come to Daneford as bishop. So, although he had met Harry at diocesan functions, he didn't have the same regard and respect for him that some of his fellow bishops, and indeed, his predecessor, had.

***

Taking the initiative, and ignoring Arthur's guidelines that only those who applied for posts should be interviewed, Harry and the other parochial nominators set off one Sunday morning to attend St. Patrick's. Of course, they stuck out like sore thumbs in the congregation—four strangers sitting together—and Steve knew immediately that here were nominators on spec! Thankfully, he'd had a well-prepared sermon and there had been a fairly full church.

Harry and his fellow nominators hung around until all the congregation had left and asked if they could have a quiet word with Steve. As the churchwardens were still in the vestry counting the collection and clearing up, Steve invited Harry and his friends over to the rectory for coffee.

"You've probably guessed that we are not looking to join your church," Harry began. "It's rather that we would like you to consider joining our church—as our new rector." Harry went on to talk about St. Saviour's, the number of parishioners, their sound finances and especially about the potential for growth and development. "Here, when you have some time, you can look at this." Harry provided a profile of the parish. "It gives a true and comprehensive description of St. Saviour's."

They got on well together, and Steve felt that they were people he could work with, so, yes, he would give St. Saviour's some thought, and if he felt it would be the right move, he would apply for the post.

"I can't promise anything," said Harry. "You know how the system works, but we would be definitely interested in you coming to St. Saviour's. My fellow nominators and I will talk further and you can feel free to give me a ring with any questions at any time." He handed Steve a business card.

Although Steve was chuffed, he knew the encounter also heralded an unsettling time for him and his wife, Fiona. They both loved the parish he was in. It was full of young families around their own age who had moved into the area when new housing had been built. They all had similar interests and there was a great sense of community and camaraderie in the parish. Fiona had her own niche in some of the parish groups, and most important of all, St. Patrick's had none of the traditional expectations of what a clergy spouse should be and do.

Fiona remembered all too well their first parish, when Steve was a curate. The rector's wife always got migraines before Mothers' Union meetings, and her health had suffered because she tried to fill too many demanding expectations.

In contrast, Fiona had freedom in St. Patrick's—and her own career as a physiotherapist, yet she sensed Steve was restless. He felt that he was coming to the end of the first phase of his ministry in St. Patrick's. The big question, he had told Fiona, was whether to wait a while and get a fresh vision for phase two, or to think of a move while he was still relatively young and fresh.

It would be a difficult decision whether or not to apply for St. Saviour's.

Chapter 11

STEVE AND FIONA had also to think of the children.

Andrew, the younger, was nearly twelve and would be starting secondary school in the autumn. That left Laura, their fifteen-year-old 'terrible teenager'. How would she take a move which would mean transferring to another school and leaving her circle of friends?

Fiona had briefly met Harry and the St. Saviour's nominators when she had brought them coffee in Steve's study. Her first impression was that they were open and friendly. She, too, had guessed who they were and why they were in St. Patrick's that morning.

After lunch, Steve and Fiona decided to take their Labrador, Barney, for a walk in the local park when they could discuss the morning's events. The arrival of four strangers at the rectory after church meant nothing to Laura and Andrew. They were used to all sorts of people calling at all sorts of hours, and they took neither notice nor interest.

"I just don't know what to make of it," said Steve, taking Fiona's hand as Barney chased in and out of the bushes. "I love being here in St. Patrick's. It has been such a rewarding time."

"I sense a 'but' coming," said Fiona. "Would I be right?"

"That's just the problem. I know I've got St. Patrick's running in much the way I want. The people are good. They're generous and committed. Well, most of them are. So why does an enquiry from St. Saviour's unsettle me and make me consider a move?

"I had a quick look at the Directory. Denis McKeever has been there for thirty years, and word has it that things are beginning to slip quite badly. But it's one of the largest parishes in Daneford, and there'd be the chance to work with a curate. They don't have a curate at the moment. Apparently, none of the ordinands was willing to go to St. Saviour's, as the rumour was quite widespread that Denis was going to retire.

"And," added Steve, "there'd be a bit of a challenge about it!"

Fiona looked at him. "You and your challenges! You know what a challenge really means? It's just another way of saying trouble and hard work! I was wondering when that restless streak in you would surface again."

They walked on in silence for a few minutes.

"And what's the rectory like? I suppose you didn't think to ask them that?"

That was another thing they liked about St. Patrick's. Before Steve had been appointed, the parish had sold the rambling old rectory and its acre of grounds to a property developer. With the proceeds, they had bought a new detached bungalow opposite the church. It was spacious yet compact. Big picture windows meant it was always bright, and being a modern build, it was well insulated and easy to heat.

There had been quite a sum left over from the sale, and that had been invested, the interest providing a cushion for parish finances. Money wasn't a major issue in St. Patrick's, and that couldn't be said of many parishes.

"Another thing," said Fiona. "Wasn't Denis McKeever's wife, what's her name, Ruby, the archetypical rector's wife who practically ran the place? I couldn't, and you know I *wouldn't* do that."

But try as he might, Steve couldn't get St. Saviour's out of his mind. He'd wake up in the small hours of the morning thinking about a move. He'd be thinking of St. Saviour's as he wrote his sermons for St. Patrick's.

Fiona was only too well aware of his turmoil, so, on the eve of their day off, she suggested to Steve that the next day they should drive over to St. Saviour's, have a look at the rectory and the church and see what the neighbourhood was like.

That evening, Steve rang Harry White to see if, by any chance, he was available to let them see the rectory and the church. He was, and a time was set. "Come to my house and I'll drive you from here. Oh, and don't wear your collar. The parish spies will be keeping their eyes peeled and we don't want rumours to start flying about!"

The first thing that struck Steve as they entered St. Saviour's was how light and bright the building seemed. Some churches had dark and oppressive atmospheres and the smell of damp hassocks and mouldy books, but St. Saviour's seemed airy. There were plenty of stained-glass windows, but somehow the light shone through them.

There had obviously been additions to the building over the years, but an interesting arrangement was that the choir stalls and organ were not at the front of the church but in a raised transept halfway down one side of the building. As Harry explained, the original church was just the present nave, but in the nineteenth century, a rector, influenced by the Oxford Movement, had decided to make the church cruciform adding on a chancel and two transepts, the smaller of which was for the choir.

"It really works," enthused Harry. "The organ and choir are very much part of the congregation, and it gives a great boost to the singing. And...we have an excellent organist and a strong choir."

Beside the church, just a few yards away, had been the old parish school, which the parish had modernised and extended as a meeting place and had connected it to the church by a foyer.

"It's great for Sunday Club and coffee after church, and it's very well used," said Harry as he showed them around. "We also have a parish hall, half a mile away, and the rectory is beside it. The hall is used for organisations such as Scouts and Guides, badminton and bowls and that sort of thing while The Old School is used more for meetings."

Back in the church vestry, Steve sneaked a look at the Preacher's Book. Clerical gossip had it that things were falling apart in St. Saviour's, but the numbers attending church were not as bad as some people were making out.

Fiona was more interested in seeing the rectory, to which Harry now brought them. It was in the same grounds as the parish hall, sharing the same entrance gate but with a separate driveway. It was a substantial square block of a house built in the early 1900s along with the hall.

As Harry led them in, Fiona's heart sank. Nothing seemed to have been done in the thirty years the McKeevers had been there. The Canon, Harry told them, was a bit of a DIY enthusiast and had never bothered too much about repairs and refurbishment being done professionally, preferring to have a go at them himself.

And it shows! Fiona thought to herself.

The wallpaper was old and flowery, and the whole house reeked of stale cigarette smoke. Both Denis and Ruby had been smokers, and the smell wasn't helped by the fact that the house had been locked up since they had retired.

The kitchen was even worse: pitted and cracked floor tiles, homemade presses topped by bright red Formica. In one corner, an ancient solid fuel stove was augmented by a dual electric ring free-standing on the counter. Two harsh fluorescent tubes hung from a high ceiling revealing steel single-glazed window frames. The whole place felt cold, damp, smelly and totally uninviting.

Steve was not the only one aware of the expression of distaste on Fiona's face. They walked around the other rooms with their worn squares of carpet edged by varnished floorboards. The bedrooms were huge and there was no en-suite.

"Of course," said Harry, as enthusiastically as he could, "the vestry have agreed that the place needs a thorough modernisation and refurbishment. I am also a glebe warden and an engineer, and we have engaged an architect to draw up the plans. Naturally, whoever is appointed will have an input before any work starts."

The garden was a good size—plenty of space for Barney—and in surprisingly good order. The garden had potential. But the rectory needed a miracle!

Chapter 12

SUSAN SHILLING SAT in the study of Revd. Peter Pearce—her Diocesan Director of Ordinands—as he tried to make sense of the Selection Conference's failure to recommend her for training.

He opened her file. "I have no doubt about the genuineness of your sense of vocation, and I stated that very clearly in my letter to the Conference. In fact, I went even further and said that I was one hundred percent behind you and thought you were just the right person to be considered for ordination. I wasn't quite as fulsome about some of the other candidates and they were accepted! So I'm really at a loss to know why the response to you wasn't positive. How did you feel the interviews went?"

"I thought they went well. The interview with the two lay people was very warm and positive, and I felt that they were really supportive."

"And what about your interview with the bishop and the cleric?" asked Peter.

There were three interviews for candidates at the Selection Conference. One interview was with two lay people, one was with a bishop and a cleric, while the third was with the director (or principal) of the Theological Institute and was mainly concerned with the candidate's academic abilities.

The first two interviews were to investigate the candidate's sense of vocation, their involvement in the Church, their beliefs and spirituality as well as their leadership potential and ability to work alongside people.

It was a tall order and well-nigh impossible to fulfil as the maximum amount of time for each interview was thirty minutes.

Peter reflected on the amount of time he gave getting to know each of the candidates from Daneford.

The organisers of the Conference tried to fit all interviews into a twenty-four-hour period, with selectors having to interview up to ten candidates in that time. How could they possibly reach considered opinions with that pressure?

No matter how much Peter complained to the organisers of the Selection Conference about the lack of time given to each candidate and the hurried nature of the process, little had changed. The selectors were meeting the candidates for the first time, and even though they were given a dossier of references and reports for each candidate, Peter knew for a fact the some selectors didn't read them beforehand, preferring to go into the interviews 'cold'.

In his own experience over a number of years, he had known candidates not recommended for matters explained in his notes to selectors, and once or twice, he had even checked these matters in advance with the Conference chairperson to make sure they would be no hindrance to the candidate. One of his candidates who had been asked to return the following year was not recommended for training over aspects of her spirituality and Church involvement for which she had been praised the previous year.

The 39 Articles state that General Councils of the Church 'may err, and sometimes have erred…', and that was certainly true of the annual Selection Conference. There was no appeal and although bishops were not bound by the recommendations, few, if any, went against them.

"I don't think my interview with the bishop went well," responded Susan. "He seemed to think that being a member of the cathedral congregation was too limited. He wanted to know if I had gone to any other styles of worship. He didn't seem to take into account that I grew up in a rural parish and so had other experiences of church. He wanted to know when I had 'made my decision for Jesus', and what were my views on homosexuality. In fact, he seemed to be obsessed by the subject! The other cleric hardly got a word in, but I felt that he, too, was a bit hard-line.

"Everything seemed fine academically. I have my degree and teacher's qualification, and there didn't seem to be any problem there."

"And how did you get on with the other candidates?" asked Peter.

"We all got on just fine. As you suggested, I moved around at meal times and there was plenty of chat."

"I just don't understand it." Some candidates Peter considered marginal got through whilst others about whom he had no doubts didn't. He realised he wasn't infallible, but...

"Of course, this is not a final 'no'," he continued. "You can go again, though you have to wait at least two years, and the bishop and myself have to agree again to put your name forward. I can only make recommendations to him. The last bishop usually went along with them, but I can't say the same about Bishop Arthur. He makes his own decisions and doesn't discuss them with me."

"I wonder..." Susan went on to tell Peter about the incident at the school, and how Laurence Finch had reported her to the bishop.

"That might have coloured the bishop's reference," Peter agreed. "I know that he was at the Conference interviewing other candidates and would have been on the committee making recommendations. Laurence Finch has a reputation throughout the diocese as being an awkward principal. He has left many casualties scattered around Lislea and further afield, but I would hope that the bishop would have known that and not let it influence his opinion of you."

As he led Susan to the door, he said, "Think about trying again. I will give you my full support. And do keep in touch."

He shut the door behind her and muttered, "Bloody Bishop!"

Chapter 13

Seriously, Arthur, we have to do something—and soon!" Sarah Easterby, Mrs. Bishop, slapped down her spoon to get her husband's attention as he scrolled through the news on his tablet. "You're not listening to a word I'm saying," she said crossly.

"Of course I am, dear."

"Then what was I saying?"

"Ah, yes, you...you were just saying, ah, yes, you were just saying how busy you are," said Arthur, with relief, smiling like a puppy that thought it should be patted!

"And?"

"And...you're run off your feet."

"No, that's not the point of what I was saying. You never listen, always caught up in your own little world!"

"Come on, now! That's a bit unfair," protested Arthur. "I was just reading the Church of England statistics on church attendance. They're really continuing to slip, you know."

Ignoring the red herring—even if it was breakfast time— Sarah fixed Arthur with beady eyes. "The point I was making is that with you so busy and me so busy, we need some help around the house. Look at the size of it. I can't keep up with trying to keep the place clean, do the washing and the cooking, and keep working. It was OK when my mother was near enough to give a hand. So...either I give up my job—which I don't want to do— or we urgently need to employ some help around the house."

Even on a bishop's stipend, which was 1.75 times that of a rector, and even though bishops were given an allowance towards a gardener and a secretary, Arthur felt that foreign holidays, having two decent cars, buying a house for retirement, not to mention what it cost to keep three teenage children, needed two incomes.

"Yes, I see your point. I totally agree." In fact, Arthur was getting tired of negotiating piles of clothes on the landing needing to be ironed. He even had to iron a shirt for himself from time to time. It would be very convenient to have someone do the laundry and to make a snack for him when he was home at lunchtime. He had noticed Sarah was getting frazzled more often and she was becoming increasingly short-tempered with him because she was so tired.

"So maybe your secretary knows of someone who might be suitable, or if not, she might put out a few feelers. It would be better than advertising. We don't want everyone knowing our business."

"Or we could go to an agency," suggested Arthur.

"It would probably be better to get someone recommended by someone we know and trust. Talk to your secretary, will you? I've got to dash. I'm late already."

With a quick peck on Arthur's cheek, she was gone.

Having graduated in law, Sarah had gone on to work in a large legal practice and had been on the verge of being made a partner when Arthur was made Bishop of Daneford. With glowing references, she had no problem getting a position in one of the leading law firms in Dublin.

She was described as a very 'savvy' lady. Good-looking, confident, intelligent and, like her father, the archdeacon, determined to get her own way—which she usually did.

If anything, she was more evangelical than Arthur. As a teenager, she had gone to Christian youth camps, and had become a leader. At university, she was a leading light in the Christian Union and had organised and led Alpha courses.

She kept Arthur true to his evangelical roots, making sure he didn't stray into what she regarded as the bland, non-challenging middle ground, or, perish the thought, any wishy-washy liberalism!

She kept him on his toes, accompanied him to as many services and functions as were possible and gave him regular critiques of his sermons. If she felt Arthur was preaching for too long, her signal to him to wind up and shut up was to take off her glasses and very ostentatiously start cleaning them. As she was usually given a seat in the front row, the message was all too clear to Arthur.

She was more understated than Mrs. Proudie of Barchester Towers, but still a force to be reckoned with.

Arthur knew he had better not forget to mention the matter of a cleaner/help to his secretary.

***

"I think I might know someone who might be suitable," said Arthur's secretary, Louise Roberts. "Her name is Lily MacDonald. She's in her early thirties. The nursing home where she worked has just closed down, and she is looking for some kind of work. Her mother isn't too well and the shorter hours would probably suit her."

"We'd be thinking along the lines of ten till three, three days a week—cleaning, washing, ironing and making a light lunch when I'm around. Maybe also preparing an evening meal? What do you think?"

"I'll certainly mention it to her, and if she's interested, then you and Sarah can interview her. She's a quiet kind of person, still single and lives with her mother. I've known her since we were in school."

"Excellent!" said Arthur. "You talk to her and we'll see how it goes from there. Now, about that address I have to give to the Mothers' Union next Friday..."

Chapter 14

H I, ANTHONY, MY old friend! This is your neighbour and newbie archdeacon, Guy Morgan!"

Anthony winced silently at the over-familiar greeting as he lifted the phone. "Oh, yes, Hello." He was going to add 'Congratulations!' but then, he wasn't going to be a hypocrite.

"The thing is," Guy continued, "I have a super proposition for you to consider. You know this new training scheme they have in the Theological Institute—the one where third-year students are placed as deacon interns in parishes? It's part of their course now."

"Yes, I did read something about it some time ago," replied Anthony.

"It's actually the bishop who allocates the parishes to have these deacon interns, but on looking at the list at our senior staff meeting…"

Anthony threw his eyes up to heaven.

"…we have just realised that St. Saviour's has been nominated. That was before Denis McKeever announced his retirement. We thought giving him a student would liven up the place! Anyway, we need to have an alternative place for next month, and as I said to Arthur, no one would better train and oversee an ordinand than you. We were actually going to nominate you first time round, but we felt St. Saviour's needed a fresh injection of life."

"I'm not sure what's involved," replied Anthony. "We don't have any accommodation to offer, and I'm not sure the vestry would agree to further expenditure."

"You don't have to worry on that score, my friend,'" Guy went on. "Accommodation will be paid from central funds. The whole scheme is cost-neutral to a parish. It's a super idea! Everybody's a winner! The deacon intern will be well trained by you, and you will have a bit of extra help. What do you think?"

"Well, I'll certainly give it some thought. How soon do you need to know?"

"ASAP. In fact, very ASAP! The institute is waiting for word. Just to fill you in—the student will be with you every Sunday and has to complete seven units of pastoral work per week in the parish, on days agreed by you and the deacon. By the way, the name of the chap we're hoping you will take is Nigel Ashurst. He's one of the more mature students. He's in his mid-fifties and is ex-Royal Navy. By all accounts, he is a really super fellow and would fit into St. Aidan's very well. Think about it overnight and ring me in the morning like a good chap." Guy rang off.

While Anthony had no desire to help either the bishop or the archdeacon out of a corner, he did rather relish having a colleague, even if only a part-time one. He would always have liked to have had a curate, but like most of the clergy outside densely populated suburban areas, he had been a one-man band for all of his ministry as a rector.

So, for selfish rather than generous reasons, he quite liked the idea and mentioned it to his wife, Annabel, over lunch.

Annabel was enthusiastic. "It would be nice to have another body to help around the parish. Goodness knows, you're well enough organised to help train someone. Only don't make them too dull and boring! If you're asking my opinion,

I say go for it! And now I've got to fly—told Lucy I'd pick up the children for her."

Anthony and Annabel were opposites in so many ways. What puzzled everyone was how he got to marry Annabel, a striking blonde, even if it was dyed nowadays, who always seemed full of life and fun. What on earth did she see in Anthony?

His contemporaries in the Theological College, as The Theological Institute was known in those days, always took time from their studies to ogle at their windows whenever Annabel came to call on Anthony. The shapely blonde walking down the drive was a distraction few could resist, especially if they were trying to get to grips with the esoteric heresies of Sabellianism.

Anthony had been an actuary before ordination—a man of order not given to spontaneity—and he and Annabel were already married when he decided to follow his vocation to be ordained. Living in a curate's house on a curate's stipend was a huge change from living in a fashionable house in a fashionable suburb on an actuary's salary. Even though Annabel did at first try to be a model clergy wife, she soon became bored and over the years had become less and less involved in parochial matters. She went to church and that was about it. She led her own life and had her own circle of friends outside of parish life.

They had one daughter, Lucy, who lived nearby, and Annabel spent more time with Lucy than at home. Luckily, her son-in-law, Chris, was tolerant and good-humoured and put up with her near-constant presence around their house.

After ordination, Anthony had become even more serious, if that were possible. He was a model curate and rector. Punctilious in visiting, exact in administration, never preaching for more than ten minutes, and he was always formally dressed in a suit and dog collar. No wonder he despaired at the sartorial inelegance of modern clergy, archdeacons included, in their fleeces, jumpers and jeans! He even preferred the old-fashioned clerical stock worn over a white shirt with proper cuffs and cufflinks.

Being overlooked for the post of archdeacon had eaten into Anthony's soul, and while he was never smiley or jokey, Annabel had noticed that he was becoming increasingly more crabby and short-tempered.

Perhaps, she thought, *having a deacon intern to train will lift him out of himself and his disappointment.*

Chapter 15

NIGEL ASHURST WAS a well-preserved fifty-six. Tall, handsome, athletic and boyish, he belied his middle-age.

He had retired as a Royal Navy captain at the age of fifty and returned to Ireland, the land of his birth, to settle with his wife in a seaside town south of Dublin where he could do some sailing. His children were grown up and married and living in the UK, where the Ashursts lived while Nigel was serving in the navy.

He always had a sense of vocation and had intended to pursue it. But just as he was finishing school, his father had died suddenly. There were lots of financial uncertainties for his mother, and he didn't want to put any more burden on his family by going to university. So he opted for his second choice of career—the Royal Navy.

Still, the sense of vocation to be ordained never went away. Like a steel splinter, it nagged away at the back of his mind. When he had settled into his new home and found a parish, he chatted to his rector about the possibility; he still had many years to offer. He went through all the usual procedures, and two years ago had entered the Theological Institute to do the three-year full-time course.

Sadly, in the June before he was due to start his studies, in an almost mirror situation to the time he was leaving school, his wife died unexpectedly and suddenly of a brain haemorrhage. He thought of postponing starting his theological course, but his children persuaded him to go ahead as planned.

Nigel accepted that if he left it any longer, it would be too late. The staff and students were very supportive, and the regular routine of life in the Institute helped him through his bereavement.

Now, he was preparing for his third year—the year when he would be made a deacon.

Nigel was disappointed when Denis McKeever retired, but was quite happy to go to Anthony Parker in St. Aidan's. He had no real preference where he should be placed and was just anxious to get started and get some pastoral experience.

The only fly in the ointment was that St. Aidan's was about fifty miles from his home beside the sea. But so had been St. Saviour's. While he enjoyed driving his Mazda MX5 convertible, it would still be a hundred-mile round trip four days a week. The Institute had told him that central funds would pay for accommodation if the distance was too great, and that was what he opted for. He would stay from Sunday morning to Wednesday afternoon in St. Aidan's, then return home where he could work on the dissertation that was a major part of the third-year programme. Nigel was well organised and determined that he wouldn't put off the dissertation until the last minute as many of the students did, leaving them stressed and having to ask for time off from their internship parishes.

However, before Nigel's internship began, the first urgent matter was to meet as soon as possible with Anthony Parker. All the other third-year students had already met with their clergy during the final training session for internship rectors. To that end, once the placement was confirmed, Nigel took the initiative and rang Anthony to set up a meeting.

***

As might be expected, the meeting was brisk and businesslike. Anthony had read up the requirements the archdeacon had emailed, and he and Nigel agreed on pastoral work for two and a half days plus Sunday services. Anthony had been told by the Institute that accommodation would be required for Nigel, and he had been able to find two possible modest houses in the parish that were for letting. With business matters concluded, Anthony went to the study door and called down the hall, "We'll have coffee now, please, dear."

Annabel had arranged to be at home that morning, anxious to see who had been allocated to St. Aidan's, and appeared a few moments later, as elegant as ever and bearing a tray.

"Ah, thank you, Annabel," said Anthony, taking the tray from her and finding a space for it on his desk. "Let me introduce you to our new deacon intern, Nigel Ashurst."

He turned to find Annabel and Nigel staring at each other.

"Annabel Price! It couldn't be! Is it really you?" gasped Nigel rising from his chair.

With equal surprise, but retaining her poise, Annabel responded, "Nigel Ashurst! Well, well, well! Anthony, you never told me it was Nigel who was coming."

"You never asked for a name, did you?" Anthony was getting flustered. "So you two know each other?"

"Indeed we do!" Annabel's smile was a little bit too knowing for Anthony's liking.

"Yes, we were at school together—in the same class, actually." Nigel tried to sound offhand.

Annabel was about to add that she and Nigel had been quite an item while at school, but bit her tongue and said instead, "You'll have to come for dinner some night. It would be good to catch up without having boring churchy business to discuss. I'll check Anthony's diary and give you a ring."

With that she departed, leaving behind just a frisson of excitement in the air.

Chapter 16

STEVE ADAMS AND his wife Fiona spent many hours discussing whether they should move from St. Patrick's—where everything was fairly cosy and going well, there were no money problems and a supportive congregation—to go to St. Saviour's just because it was a bigger parish and would have a curate and provide Steve with the new challenge he felt he needed.

If the decision were solely his, he'd have said 'yes' without a second thought. But he had Fiona to consider, and Andrew and Laura. Andrew would be leaving primary school anyway, so a move to a new school was going to happen, although if they stayed, Andrew would still be with his pals. Going to a new school in a new area could be daunting enough, even for such an easy-going and friendly young lad as he was.

Laura, however, was another matter.

Without mentioning where or when, Steve and Fiona had broached a possible move to her after dinner one night.

"A move to a new area?" Already there was fire in Laura's eyes.

"Well, yes, possibly," Steve replied carefully. "But a nice area—a bit like the one we're in now."

"Then why bother?" Laura asked with devastating logic.

"It's just the way things are in the Church," Fiona tried to mollify her. "Clergy move parishes from time to time, all the time. Your dad thinks that maybe that time has come for us."

There was silence, just for a few seconds, and then Laura erupted. "You never think of me, do you? Oh, no! I just don't count, do I? You never think how it is going to affect me and my

54

friends!" Shooting a venomous look at Steve, she cried, "I suppose you've worked hard to persuade Mum. What about her job and her friends? No, it's always just about you and your precious job—what *you* want—in spite of all that crap that you preach!"

Laura got up from the table, stamped out of the room and slammed the kitchen door after her, shattering the two bottom panes of glass and making Barney leap from his bed in fright.

Steve looked at Fiona in despair.

"Leave her to me." Fiona laid her hand on Steve's arm. "I'll go up and talk to her later. She'll calm down. Just you see."

Steve headed off to his study. He had a school assembly to prepare for the morning. It was the last thing he wanted to do, but what choice did he have? He sat at his desk, head in his hands, completely confused and completely fed up.

The phone rang. He wasn't in any humour to talk to anyone. He let it ring until his clergy conscience got the better of him and he lifted the receiver.

"St. Patrick's Rectory. Steve Adams."

"Ah, Steve, this is Harry White from St. Saviour's."

Not now, prayed Steve. *Please don't ask me for a definite yes or no at this particular moment.*

"I don't know how to put this…" Harry White was clearly uncomfortable. "I'm afraid there's been a hiccup in the nomination process."

Harry outlined what the bishop had said to him and how it was going to delay an appointment being made, and that once the three months had elapsed, it would be the bishop's right to make an appointment.

"I'm terribly sorry about this. I really am. But I'd like you to know that you were the first choice of the nominators from St. Saviour's. We really think you are the right person for our parish—that is, if you would have come, of course. But this has completely thrown us.

"I'm going to be honest with you. I feel that Bishop Easterby has pulled a fast one on us, and I'm sorry to say, once he has the decision to himself, he won't go along with what we suggest. I feel really let down. I've been around Church matters for quite a long time, and I've got to tell you that I've never felt as gutted and as disillusioned as I do right now. Bloody bishop—if you'll pardon the French!"

Steve didn't know whether to laugh or cry. In one sense, he was relieved, but in another sense, he was deeply disappointed.

"Thanks for letting me know. In fact, Fiona and I were still discussing whether we should consider a move. But now the decision has been made for us. Thanks for all your time and confidence in me."

"I wish I could say maybe another time," said Harry. "But unless something happens to our bloody bishop—now there's a thought—I can't really see that I'll be able to invite you to consider St. Saviour's again.

'I'm really sorry for causing such an unsettling time for you and Fiona. I can only thank you for your interest and wish you well in the future. Maybe our paths will cross again?" Saying a quick goodbye, Harry hung up.

Was it God's will? Steve didn't believe in those who said such things were 'meant to be'. That, in his opinion, was a cop out. The real reason was more likely to be found in the unpredictable nature of being human, not to mention a certain *bloody bishop*.

He got up to tell Fiona. Was it good news or bad news?

Chapter 17

L ILY MACDONALD DROVE her ageing Nissan Micra along one of the leafy suburban roads of Daneford, looking out for numbers on gate posts. There were more grand sounding names than numbers, she noticed. The See House was number 14, and thankfully it was clearly marked. The gateway was open, but she thought it might be a bit presumptuous to bring her battered car up the bishop's driveway, so she parked outside on the road.

Her interview with Bishop Easterby and his wife was at 7:30 p.m. She had left herself plenty of time, so she sat in the car and checked her Facebook page to while away a few minutes.

Well, here I am, she reflected to herself, *thirty-two years of age and what have I done with my life? Not a lot! Just going from one skivvy's job to another!*

Lily was an only child. Her father, Fred, had died when she was only six. She hardly remembered him. He was much older than her mother; that much was evident from the photographs of her parents dotted throughout the house. She realised she knew very little about her father, and her mother had not talked much about him. All Lily knew was that her mother was quite young when Lily was born, but she didn't know how her parents had met.

Once Lily started secondary school, her mother had gone back to work part-time to ease things financially. Her mother had not been able to afford the mortgage repayments on the house she and Fred had bought, so after his death, they had moved into a ground-floor flat in what had been a large town house in a once well-to-do area. The houses looked imposing but they were all sub-divided.

Most of the money her father had left had been eaten away by the rent. So, apart from anything else, it was a necessity for her mother to work. Her widow's pension kept them afloat, just about. When school fees had to be found, there were Church charities to call upon.

Lily was grateful for the sacrifices her mother had made, and on leaving school, she made up her mind to get a job and start earning rather than think of going to college. At least that way, she could contribute towards the rent and food.

Alas, jobs were not plentiful, and she drifted into working for care institutions. As she had no nursing qualifications, she became a sort of general factotum, helping nurses when needed—they always seemed to be short-staffed—and doing general cleaning work, looking after the laundry and helping to serve meals.

By her early twenties, her mother and she were more like sisters than parent and child. They socialised together and even went on holidays together, including a few package holidays to Greece and the Canaries.

Her mother kept urging Lily to get qualified as a nurse: *"One day you'll be on your own, and you'll need a decent salary—unless you marry someone who will be able to keep you!"*

But while Lily had had some boyfriends, the relationships never came to anything. 'Two's company and three's a crowd', as they say, and it seemed to her boyfriends that to take Lily on meant taking on her mother as well!

So life, for Lily, just drifted on. And then five years ago, her mother found a lump on her breast which turned out to be malignant. She had a mastectomy and then started radiotherapy. All seemed to go well, but then later tests showed that the cancer was back—in her lungs and pancreas, for which she was receiving chemotherapy.

Recently, her mother had become increasingly tired and had to give up work. Then the care home that Lily worked in closed. So now, she needed to find work to pay the rent, but not full-time work or else she wouldn't have time to care for her mother.

When her friend, Louise Roberts, Arthur's secretary, told her about the job in the See House, Lily was keen and was sure it would suit her well…if she got it.

And here she was for her interview.

With two minutes to 7:30 p.m., she got out of the car and walked up the short avenue to the rather imposing red-brick mansion that served as the Bishop of Daneford's residence. It was rather like the house where she and her mother had their flat—two storeys over a basement—but the See House had spacious gardens around it and ample car parking space at the front for Arthur's and Sarah's BMWs.

As she ascended the granite steps to the front door, Lily noticed that the double garage to her right had been converted into an office for the bishop and his secretary.

She rang the bell and waited. The door was opened by Sarah Easterby.

"Ah, you must be Lily MacDonald, and bang on time. I'm Sarah Easterby. Do please come in. My husband will join us in a minute. He's in his office. I'll ring through to him." Sarah lifted the phone on the hall table, dialled an internal number and summoned Arthur.

The hallway was rather dark, not helped by gloomy portraits of previous bishops of Daneford, which hung around the walls and up the stairs.

Lily was brought into a bright, spacious sitting room, tastefully decorated, and shown to an armchair.

Arthur joined them almost immediately. Lily couldn't help feeling that they made a handsome couple, but they were somewhat formal and aloof.

Louise Roberts had obviously filled in the Easterbys about Lily, and the interview was rather brief.

Sarah took the lead. "I think Miss Roberts has told you what's involved. We're looking for help three days a week from ten 'til three. It will involve cleaning and hoovering, washing and ironing, making a light lunch for the bishop when he's here, and preparing an evening meal which can be left in the oven or ready to be microwaved."

"Yes," Lily replied, "Louise told me, and that's all right with me."

They discussed wages, which, although not generous, were just above the minimum wage.

"Let me show you around the house," suggested Sarah. "Arthur, you can go back to your office if you like. Is there anything else you want to ask Miss MacDonald?"

"I suppose just 'when can you start'?" replied Arthur.

"I'm free at the moment. I could start next Monday if you wish."

"Capital!" said Arthur. "Is that OK with you, dear?" he asked Sarah.

"Yes, that would be ideal. Now," she said to Lily, "come with me."

The hall was the darkest place in the house, but all the other rooms were bright, and all had been refurbished for the Easterbys, as had happened with every move they made. The kitchen was also new, and there were patio doors which led into the well-tended garden.

It'll be a pleasant place to work, thought Lily. She only hoped the occupants would be the same.

Chapter 18

SUSAN SHILLING'S FAILURE to be recommended for ordination training hurt her more deeply than she realised was possible. And, yes, if she was honest, it had undermined her faith. It was her vocation, not a passing whim, and both the cathedral clergy and the Diocesan Director of Ordinands had encouraged her.

She wasn't sure she was up for applying to go to Selection Conference again. If one rejection had made her feel so fragile, what would a second rejection do? And if Arthur Easterby was still Bishop of Daneford in two years' time, that's exactly what would happen. Once the bishop felt you had crossed him or done something he didn't agree with, he remembered and was unforgiving to the end. Bloody bishop, indeed!

She was still profoundly unhappy in St. Olaf's School. Laurence Finch continued to freeze her out and gave her no encouragement, reprimanding her for any minor mistake or breach of discipline in her class. Now she thought about it, the bishop and the principal were in many ways alike.

Her only support was Robbie, her boyfriend. Robbie owned a car sales and repair business, and they'd been together for two years. She'd told him everything and didn't feel at all guilty that whenever Arthur Easterby took his car in to be serviced, Robbie wasn't as generous with the bill as he might have been, had Arthur treated Susan better.

Even though the house Susan was buying was a small, two-bedroomed terrace house, paying the mortgage didn't leave much for living it up. She'd considered taking in a lodger, which would help with the bills, but she loved having the place to herself, especially when Robbie was there: the house was too small for any privacy.

Several times recently Robbie had brought up moving in and said he'd be happy to share the mortgage payments, but with the Selection Conference coming up, she didn't want to be put on the spot if she was asked about her living arrangements. It was a bit silly of her, she knew. So many couples lived together—including some of the Fellowship of Vocation.

Coming from the country, she was perhaps more aware of the gossip such arrangements caused, but times had changed, even in the rural areas it was hardly remarked on anymore. Still, with the Selection Conference coming up, she didn't want to compromise her chances.

But really, what was to stop her? She wasn't going to offer herself for ordination again, that was for sure. So Robbie might as well move in and help out financially.

They'd talked about getting engaged and put it off in case she was accepted for training as she'd have been living in the Theological Institute. Robbie still lived with his parents, and marriage would be difficult living apart, so they'd decided to wait until she was ordained and in a curacy where a house would be provided. But now?

Sod the Church and the bloody bishop! The time for sacrifice is over!

She would still go to church, of course, but she was going to leave the cathedral. They knew about her Selection Conference rejection, and she didn't want to be known as a failed ordinand.

She would go to Wendy Morris's church, St. Olaf's. It would mean seeing school parents, but she liked Wendy, who came to do a weekly assembly—Susan had noticed how unfriendly the headmaster had been towards Wendy since that incident about the Stones' children.

Well, that made two of them, and there were more people around Lislea, past and present, who had dared to stand up to Laurence Finch, and who had been vilified by him ever since.

Susan would bide her time and see if any vacancies came up in other schools in Lislea or the surrounding area. She was confident Wendy would give her a good reference, and Laurence's reputation was well known among the teaching fraternity, although few, if any, would take him on.

While she'd been looking forward to the pastoral side of ministry particularly, she realised now that she could fulfil that aspect of her vocation by volunteering as a Samaritan or getting involved in a charity.

It was time to turn over a new leaf and enjoy herself.

Chapter 19

STAFF MEETINGS WITH Anthony Parker in St. Aidan's Rectory were brisk and brief, seldom lasting more than half an hour. They started at nine a.m. and finished at nine-thirty—far too early for Annabel to appear. She spent that time putting on make-up, doing her hair and deciding which outfit to wear, so there was no chance of her appearing with coffee and fawning over Nigel.

Training rectors were supposed to have a more informal meeting with their interns once a month to give them the opportunity of discussing in-depth how they were experiencing ministry, any personal matters, ups and downs and that sort of thing. But that wasn't Anthony's style.

Anthony ended the staff meeting with the Grace, and then asked Nigel if he had a minute. "Annabel is anxious to organise this dinner she mentioned. My diary is very full. The only night I can make is Saturday. I know it would mean an extra drive for you, but if we made it early, say six-thirty p.m. for seven, how would that suit? I don't do late Saturday nights. If it doesn't suit, never mind!"

"What I could do is come up Saturday instead of Sunday and stay the night in the rented house. Yes, Saturday evening will be fine. I look forward to it."

Nigel was shown to the door to get on with the list of tasks and visits he had been given for the week.

Saturday came. Nigel showered after a strenuous game of tennis that afternoon and wondered what to wear to the rectory. He didn't think Anthony ever did 'smart casual'. No doubt he would be wearing a suit and clerical collar.

Nigel decided on a blazer and chinos, white shirt and naval tie. It always seemed to impress.

Parking his MX5 in the rectory drive, he rang the doorbell just after 6:30 p.m. As expected, Anthony opened the door in his clericals. Annabel, blonde and tanned, shimmered up the hall in a low-cut, pale-green dress, a large emerald on a gold chain around her neck.

Handing Anthony a bottle of good wine, Nigel gave Annabel a bunch of flowers.

"Oh, how sweet of you!" she said, kissing him on the cheek. "Now, you must have a gin and tonic. Don't mind Anthony, he never touches the stuff, but after slaving in the kitchen all day, I certainly need one!"

The two men sat in the lounge, Anthony with an orange juice and Nigel with his G&T, making stilted conversation. Thankfully, it didn't have to go on too long as Annabel called them for dinner.

"I hope you don't mind eating in the kitchen? As there are only three of us, it seemed a bit too formal to use the dining room, and—" she flashed a smile at Nigel "—we're among old friends!"

The kitchen was the width of the rectory and bright and airy. Annabel had obviously put pressure on Anthony—or used her considerable charm on the glebe wardens, probably the latter—to get a modern kitchen with French doors leading out to a patio.

Nigel found Anthony to be quite a mixture, theologically speaking—conservative on some issues, liberal on others— but whatever opinion he held, it was held with conviction.

He was like the way he dressed: black and white with no concessions in between.

That was not to say that he couldn't, or hadn't changed his opinions on some matters.

He had been staunchly against the remarriage of divorced persons in church until his daughter's marriage had broken up after two short years. Their daughter was too like Annabel, with a wild, daring streak, and her husband was too like Anthony. As Annabel often mused to herself, she would also have broken up with Anthony shortly after their marriage, but those were different times and she had no real career, so she put up with him and carved out her own life.

Anthony had equally been opposed to the ordination of women, in spite of Annabel being a fervent supporter—or was Anthony against it because Annabel was for it?—but when General Synod passed the necessary bills, he had accepted that decision of the Church, though in his heart of hearts he was still unconvinced and certainly would not have taken a female deacon intern.

Inevitably, the conversation around the table was all about Church.

"I deplore today's lack of discipline in liturgy and robes. Everybody seems to do what they like and wear what they like. We're losing our identity as a Church and we are, in some places, indistinguishable from Rome at one end of the spectrum, or from the Baptists at the other. And, I'm sorry to say, our bishop is doing nothing about it. He seems to be the lap dog of that terrible new archdeacon, Guy Morgan, who, I regret to say, doesn't wear robes either, in spite of his senior position. Our people in many parishes don't know what they are or what they stand for!"

Nor does the Theological Institute always enforce the canons, thought Nigel, but decided not to add fuel to the fire.

Annabel sighed audibly. "Anthony, you're such a grumpy old man! I'm sure Nigel is bored with all this churchy talk. I certainly am! Now, what I want to know is what my former, em, school friend has been up to these last thirty-five years, and what has made our paths cross after all this time."

Turning to Anthony, she said, "Be a dear and make some coffee—not instant, use the cafetière. And top up our glasses. Nigel has a lot of interesting stuff to tell me. Let's move back into the lounge."

Annabel ignored Anthony's less than subtle look at his watch as she took Nigel's arm and sat down beside him on the sofa.

Chapter 20

Monday, Wednesday and Friday, from ten a.m. to three p.m., were agreed as the days and times Lily MacDonald would work for the Easterbys. Sarah had taken a few hours off work to show Lily where the hoover was kept, how to use the washing machine and dishwasher, where clothes for washing would be left, how Arthur's episcopal rochet was to be ironed etc. etc. Lily was also given a key to the See House and shown how to use the burglar alarm.

For the first—and last—time, she made Lily a cup of coffee. Arthur was at Church House for a morning of meetings.

"The bishop will have his elevenses in his office when he's at home but likes to have his lunch in the kitchen. He will leave you a calendar to let you know when he's here and when he's away. I'll leave things like soup and rolls and cold meat, but you might ask him what he would like for lunch when you bring him his coffee at eleven a.m.

"His secretary, Miss Roberts, whom I believe you know, usually brings her own sandwiches for lunch and has them in her office. You can have your lunch in the kitchen when the bishop has finished his. He usually only allows himself half an hour at lunchtime.

"It would be a great help if you could prepare a casserole or something like that before you go home. Something we can put in the microwave in the evening. If you leave a list of what you need—preferably a week in advance—I will see that it's left in the fridge.

"I think that is probably all for now. Here's my mobile phone number if you need me—but only if it's really important. And perhaps you can give me yours. Now I really have to fly."

Lily sat down, mesmerised by all the instructions she had received. At least her friend Louise would be near at hand if she needed any advice.

She looked at the clock—eleven a.m. Would the bishop be back from Church House? Was he waiting for his coffee? She had better go and check.

Sarah had shown her the door from the utility room leading down some stairs to the double garage that served as offices for Arthur and Louise. The first office was Arthur's, and only he used the stairs to the house. The front of the offices had two ceiling-to-floor windows separated by a door—the main door for Louise's office, which included a waiting area from which there was a door into Arthur's office. The two offices were separated by a stud wall partition. However, if Louise concentrated enough, she could hear most of what went on in the bishop's office, and that, of course, made her job much more interesting. There was little she didn't know about Daneford diocese and its clergy!

Lily descended the stairs from the main house and knocked on the bishop's office door. There was no answer, so she tried the handle and found it was unlocked; she tentatively opened the door and found his office empty. *He must still be at Church House.*

Going through the door that led into Louise's office, she startled her friend, who was busy working on her computer.

"Tra La! Here I am," said Lily spreading her arms out as if she were on stage.

"Jesus!" exclaimed Louise. "You gave me a fright!"

"Are you allowed to use language like that in here, of all places?" asked Lily in mock shock.

"Actually, no!" smirked Louise. "Thankfully, you weren't the bishop, although he usually makes more noise coming into his office. You sneaked in like a little mouse. Have you had your meeting with Mrs. Bishop?"

"Yes, I've been given the whole rundown. Hope I can remember it all. I can tell you, it's going to be busy, trying to squeeze it all into five hours, three days a week."

"Oh, they like to get their money's worth," replied Louise. "They're not bad, I suppose, but you couldn't call them friendly. They think they're a cut above the likes of you and me."

"Well, me, anyway," said Lily. "I'm only the skivvy. But it suits at the moment with Mum so ill."

"Listen," said Louise, "I know the bishop won't be back until after lunch. He's at a series of meetings. I organise his diary, so I know his whereabouts. Let's break the rules from the beginning and go up to their kitchen for a cup of coffee. I'll put on the answerphone. I know he won't be ringing. You know, I've been working here for three years and I haven't once been in the house. I'd love a snoop around, and you can be my guide!"

Chapter 21

I F SUSAN SHILLING was feeling the brunt of Laurence Finch's antagonism, so too was Revd. Wendy Morris, Rector of St. Olaf's and chairperson of the school's board of management.

When Wendy was appointed to St. Olaf's parish, she was told by some of her colleagues that Laurence Finch was a difficult principal to work with. But while Wendy noted what they said, she wasn't one to let the rumours colour her future relationship with the principal. She preferred to start with a clean sheet and make up her own mind.

At her previous parish, her predecessor insisted on meeting her and filling her in on who to watch out for and who might be troublesome and so on. All negative stuff. After the first year, she decided that the dire warnings of her predecessor reflected more on him than on the parishioners he was telling her about.

So that's the way she approached Laurence Finch, and for the first few months, they had an amicable working relationship.

But the first signs of a strain came when Jonathan Stewart, the honorary treasurer of the school board, came to discuss the accounts with Wendy before the AGM.

"The accounts are all fine, except for one little anomaly," he said. "There are a few fundraising events held during the year, and the proceeds go into the principal's account rather than the board's. Laurence Finch is the only signatory on that account, but no record of that account appears on the financial statement I present to the AGM. It's been like that for years, but since I took over as honorary treasurer, I haven't been very happy about it.

"I have no doubts about Laurence Finch's honesty, and I know he uses it for extras and special items, saying he doesn't want to be bothering me every time something has to be purchased. But I would rather that the board gave him whatever sum he thinks he needs as petty cash, and that the proceeds of the events be recorded in the school's financial statement. It means that parents can see what was raised at each particular event."

Jonathan's suggestion seemed a more transparent way of handling things, and Wendy agreed.

"I don't mind suggesting this to Laurence sometime before the AGM," continued Jonathan. "It wouldn't be right to bring it up at the meeting without him knowing in advance, nor would it be fair. But I'm an accountant, and I like everything to be open and transparent. I just wanted to have your agreement before mentioning it."

And that was that—until Wendy went in to take assembly the following day. Or, more accurately, *after* Wendy had taken assembly.

It was her usual practice to go into Laurence's office following assembly each week to discuss school business. Sometimes there was little to discuss and the meeting was short. It all depended on what was coming up or if there had been any incidents.

But that morning, there was a definite air of tension in the office. Laurence glowered at Wendy from behind his desk. "So you don't trust me with school money, is that it? Do you think I am dishonest? Never before in all my time have I had a rector who doubted or meddled in the way I run my school. I must say, I am very disappointed, and very annoyed, at both you and Jonathan Stewart, colluding together against me." A vein throbbed in his temple.

No matter what way Wendy tried to explain their proposal— well, it was Jonathan's, actually, but she wasn't going to distance herself from the honorary treasurer—as good accounting and not personal, there was no mollifying Laurence Finch, who did indeed take it very personally.

"I will resign rather than change the way I run my school," he thundered, "and I will make sure that everyone knows who's to blame. How will that look for you?"

Wendy and Jonathan had a brief chat that evening and both decided that it wasn't worth the fight or the fallout. In spite of his fiery temper and tetchiness, Laurence ran a good school. The matter was dropped.

But the foundation of a tempestuous relationship between principal and rector had been laid.

In some ways, Wendy was glad she was single. If she had children in the school, she knew they wouldn't have an easy time in the light of her new strained relationship with Laurence.

Even before that, there had been the incident concerning the admission of Jake and Joshua Stone. Wendy had been determined that she wouldn't give in on a matter of principle, not to mention pastoral responsibility.

But after two clashes, Laurence cancelled any further after-assembly meetings with Wendy; he now communicated with her only through email or the school secretary. Board meetings became tense affairs with everyone watching their Ps and Qs, and Wendy stuck strictly to the rule book.

The morning of the AGM, three parents came to see Wendy, and her heart sank. This could only be more trouble.

One of the after-school activities which the parents' association funded was a drama class. Laurence himself was very keen on drama and was a member of the Lislea Little Theatre Group, where he was a regular member of the cast. He was very proud of the fact that he was encouraging an interest in acting and hoped that one day the school could claim its own celebrity. But attendance at the heavily subsidised class had dwindled, and a growing number of parents felt that their money would be better used in providing some sporting activities, like soccer for the boys and hockey for the girls.

They were going to bring the matter up at the AGM that evening and wanted Wendy's support. Would she have a chat with the principal about it today?

"I understand what you are saying. But I, as chairperson of the board, have no official function at the AGM. It's really a parents' meeting. I attend only as an observer. You would be better speaking with Mr. Finch about it yourselves."

Wendy was very definitely not going to be drawn into another clash with Laurence.

"Oh, we're not so sure how he would take it. And, you know, he's not the easiest to talk to, and we don't want him to fly off the handle if he disagrees. We've got children in the school. So, we thought…" They looked pleadingly at Wendy.

"Sorry, I have to say no. This is something for the parents' association to bring up if they feel so strongly about it. But I'm afraid that I can do nothing."

Good grief, she thought to herself after she let them out, *is there no relief in this job?*

Chapter 22

A ND HOW WAS bishop-ing going for Arthur? And his clergy?
Well, they had to admit, he was efficient, especially when
compared to his predecessor, old Bill Grace.

Emails pinged regularly into the computers of the clergy of
Daneford, announcing diocesan dates, giving instructions about
how confirmations were to be arranged and about courses and
seminars on Church growth coming up. His latest email caused
a bit of a stir among his hard-pressed clergy. It was, as announced
at the recent Diocesan Council, that Archdeacon Guy Morgan
would be introducing MDRs in the very near future.

"What on earth are MDRs?" exclaimed one puzzled cleric,
and then read on. Puzzlement gave way to horror! An MDR was
a Ministerial Development Review, to be conducted annually by
the archdeacon himself.

Guy was now known amongst the clergy as 'Super Guy', and
it wasn't meant as a compliment. Guy peppered his conversations
with 'super': comments that met with his approval were 'super';
everything he suggested would be 'super'—even the changeable
Irish weather was 'super'! Though to the ultra-cynics like
Anthony, he was 'superficial'!

But MDRs! More form-filling, more introspection!
Bloody bishop! Bloody archdeacon! The clergy of Daneford
were summoned to a breakfast meeting to explain it all in
Super Guy's super Parish Hall. Funerals began to be requested
in many parishes for that morning.

As for Arthur, up close and personal—it was early days, but many of the clergy were getting the impression that he was more of an ideas man than a pastoral bishop. When he did meet with his clergy, he was more interested in what was going on in their parishes than in how they and their families were getting on.

Wendy Morris's experience of Arthur as a bishop was not a happy one, and it all had to do with the school.

She had attended the school AGM and had very much taken a back seat, as she usually did. Really her only function was to say thanks to the principal and staff at the end of the meeting—if someone else hadn't done so already.

Usually, the AGMs were placid affairs. Laurence was adept at fixing elections beforehand, and he made sure no 'troublemakers' were appointed who might question how he ran the school.

But, of course, these so-called 'troublemakers' were eligible to attend the AGM, and he was always a bit stressed and tetchy before the event.

Knowing what Laurence was like, very few parents were prepared to bring up anything controversial—except for that night! One of the three parents who had come to see Wendy got up under Any Other Business and suggested that, in her opinion—which, she said, was supported by a growing number of parents—after-school drama classes should be replaced by sporting activities, which would be a better use of parents' association money.

A small minority wanted drama classes to continue, as did Laurence Finch, but there was clearly a big majority in favour of sport. Before a vote was called for, the chairperson, seeing Laurence's face getting redder and redder and the telltale throbbing of a vein in his temple, addressed Wendy, who was sitting in the back row.

"Reverend Morris, what do you think we should do?"

Wendy stood up and said, "I'm not a parent, and this is a decision for parents. I have no opinion one way or the other." She quickly sat down.

The vote was taken, with a big majority in favour of sport.

The meeting was going to end with an uneasy atmosphere in the room, so Wendy stood up and thanked Mr. Finch for running such a successful school. She went on to say how lucky the school was, not only in the facilities that were provided but also because they had a very talented and committed staff. And then she said a closing prayer.

Laurence didn't stay for the tea afterwards and abruptly left the hall.

Two days later, Wendy was in for her usual weekly assembly. At the end of it, Laurence asked her to step into his office. His face was like thunder and he clearly hadn't got over the AGM's decision about sport, which he had taken as a personal challenge to his authority. Wendy was glad that at least she had had no part in it.

In that she was mistaken!

"So, once again you have tried to undermine me. This time in public! I would have thought that you would have supported both me and the staff. We all feel very let down by you and had expected more. The teachers are all trained in PE. It is part of the curriculum, yet you didn't take that into account with your remarks. They all feel abandoned by you as chairperson of the school board."

"Come on, now," Wendy protested. "Did you not hear what I said—and also what I didn't say? I gave no opinion. I took no side."

"That's not how it appeared to me—or to the staff. And, further, I know you aided and abetted three parents in bringing the matter up. They were seen coming out of your house.

I would have expected more loyalty, but I should have learnt by now!"

Nothing Wendy said could persuade Laurence otherwise. She left the school visibly shaken, not only by Laurence's false accusations, but also by the way he had turned the staff against her. And how had he known who had been to see her? The school was nowhere near the rectory.

Relations with Laurence and the school were deteriorating fast.

That evening, having mulled over the implications all day, she decided to ring Arthur, as both her bishop and patron of the school, to alert him of the situation.

"Ah, yes," said Arthur after Wendy had finished, "I am aware of the situation. I had Mr. Finch here to see me yesterday. I've asked the archdeacon to meet you and to see how this sad matter can be resolved."

Wendy put down the phone, dumbfounded and furious. Her bishop had had a visit from her school principal complaining about her, and yet he had never lifted the phone to ask her side of the story. What kind of episcopal support was that? And sending the archdeacon to quiz her! The principal could see the bishop, but one of his clergy could only be seen by the archdeacon.

Bloody bishop! Is that the way he was going to treat his hard-pressed clergy?

Chapter 23

As the weeks passed by, Anthony Parker became more and more bad-humoured. He was pleased, in spite of himself, with Nigel Ashurst, his deacon intern. He couldn't fault Nigel's pastoral ability or diligence. He did as he was asked and didn't duck out of any responsibilities or duties. Nor could Anthony complain about Nigel's preaching and conduct of services.

No, his bad humour sprang from Annabel's fawning around Nigel and how she would, in an over-familiar way, touch his arm. Then there were the in-jokes about the past and mutual friends whom Anthony didn't know. He was annoyed by her coquettish behaviour and felt sidelined.

Anthony guessed that Annabel and Nigel had gone out with each other in school, after which their paths diverged when Nigel joined the Royal Navy and left the country. But, it seemed to Anthony, that Annabel still had a place for Nigel in her heart.

If Anthony could have analysed himself—which he couldn't— he would have seen that he was acutely jealous of Nigel. But not being able to recognise that, it expressed itself in tetchiness and bad humour.

Annabel had started to get up earlier on those mornings when there were staff meetings, and she would linger at the door of the kitchen to offer Nigel a cup of coffee before he left.

One morning, Anthony waited until Nigel had left and then challenged her. "I wish you wouldn't hang around after staff meetings, offering Nigel coffee and making all those silly jokes.

You're acting like a lovesick schoolgirl. It's unbecoming and immature!"

"There, there!" Annabel put on her best 'mother' voice. "Is my poor little Anthony's nose all out of joint?" There was no mistaking the mockery and sarcasm in her tone.

Anthony felt a surge of anger, which he found almost impossible to control. His face reddened. He clenched and unclenched his fists.

The moment passed, but it seemed an age to Anthony.

Avoiding eye contact, he made for the front door. "I've got work to attend to, and I don't know whether I'll be back or not for lunch."

With that, he was gone.

Annabel sat down at the table and smiled to herself, gratified that she had provoked such an angry response from her dull husband.

After a leisurely breakfast, she dressed and decided to head into town and do some shopping.

She found herself taking a circuitous route to the town centre, past the house the church had rented for Nigel. One part of her mind told her it was a silly thing to do, but another more insistent voice was egging her on.

She saw Nigel's MX5 in the driveway.

The voice in her head told her to call. She parked behind his car, went to the front door and rang the bell.

"Hello, Annabel!" said Nigel. "What brings you to my humble pad?"

"Oh, I was just wondering if the accommodation they provided you with is OK. You know Anthony. He would think anything would do. I just wanted to make sure that it was comfortable and adequate."

"Well, yes, it is actually. Why don't you come in and have a look around?"

It was very neat and tidy. Nigel's navy training saw to that.

"Have you time for a coffee? Or must you get back for Anthony's lunch?" asked Nigel.

"I have time," smiled Annabel. "Anthony's away for the day. At all sorts of meetings, I suppose."

They sat in the kitchen drinking coffee, talking about this and that and spending a very pleasant hour.

What neither of them realised was that Anthony had also intended to visit Nigel to sort out some details about the following Sunday's service but had got delayed on a call. And, as he was later than he had planned, he saw Annabel's car in Nigel's driveway.

Seething with rage, he drove home and waited for her to return. It was a long wait because after leaving Nigel, Annabel had gone on to do some shopping.

The wait did nothing for Anthony's peace of mind, nor for his sense of betrayal. His imagination was working overtime, and, as more time passed, he convinced himself that Annabel was having an affair with her old boyfriend, his deacon intern.

As Annabel opened the front door, she was confronted in the hallway by the contorted, red face of Anthony.

"I know where you've been. I know what you've been up to. You can take that smile off your face. You're nothing but a common slut!"

"Oh, come on, Anthony!" Annabel's smile and dancing eyes seemed to mock him further. "You're imagining things! In fact—"

Her explanation was never uttered, as Anthony's fist smashed into her face, knocking her off her feet, leaving her a crumpled heap on the floor.

She never heard the front door slam as Anthony left and drove off with a screech of tyres.

Chapter 24

Lᴵᴸʏ MᴀᴄDᴏɴᴀʟᴅ ᴡᴀs settling into her job in the See House. On arriving in the morning, she found that the best way to check whether the bishop was going to need coffee and/or lunch was to ask Louise in the bishop's office. If Arthur was in for the morning, then contact between Lily and Louise was brief. But if he wasn't there, they would arrange to have coffee together in Louise's office, and if he was away all day, Louise would bring her lunch up to the See House kitchen.

Arthur was away on a bishops' retreat for a few days, so there wasn't any chance of being caught as Lily and Louise sat around the kitchen table over lunch.

"And how's your mother these days?" asked Louise. "I've been meaning to call around."

"She's not great at the moment. Her breathing isn't good, and any exertion takes it out of her. She spends more and more time in bed, where she has an oxygen tank and mask. She can be in quite a lot of pain, and she has painkillers when she needs them, and sleeping tablets for nighttime."

"Oh, I am sorry. It all seems so unfair. She was...I mean, she *is* such a sweet person, and she's had it hard enough all her life from what you have told me, what with your father dying so long ago. Life can be such a bitch! She's lucky to have you."

"The doctors are not so sure how long she will be able to stay at home, and they are already mentioning the possibility of hospice care. But I'm there most of the time—apart from

82

the few hours here—so being with her is not such a problem. It's just if the pain and her breathing get worse, the hospice would be able to make her more comfortable. Mum won't think that far down the line. She refuses to talk about her illness and always changes the subject if I ask her how she's feeling."

"That must be really difficult," replied Louise sympathetically.

"It's just hard to know what to do," said Lily. "Both of us try to put on a brave face and be optimistic without mentioning 'the elephant in the room'."

Realising that not a lot more could be said, Louise decided to change the subject. "And how are you getting on with the bishop? Do you know what his nickname is? Arse! That's what all the clergy call him. Well, most of them. It comes from his initials— Arthur Ronald Stephen Easterby. Apparently, he's been called that since he was a student!"

Lily laughed. "And I suppose you could say he is a bit up his own…arse, too. He's not the most friendly—he doesn't seem to be able to make small talk. Though, at times, when I'm making his lunch, I find him looking at me. It's a bit unnerving, as he doesn't say anything. I hope he's not one of those randy vicar types you read about in the tabloids!"

"Oh, I don't think so. Though I did hear that he had an eye for the girls when he was in college. It's surprising what some of the clergy tell me when they're waiting in my office! There's not much I don't know about the clergy of Daneford—and beyond! But I wouldn't worry because if he put a foot—or a hand—wrong, Mrs. Bishop would have his whatnots cut off! He's just a bit moody and outside of his public persona a bit of an introvert."

"I'm probably just imagining it," Lily confessed. "It's just he says so little."

"Now there are one or two of the clergy who can get a bit touchy-feely and over-familiar. There's one in particular who gives me the creeps, always passing remarks on what I'm wearing and telling me that I 'look very fit'! One time, his arms brushed against my boobs, and he winked and said, 'Oh, that was nice!'—the creep! Now I always make sure to keep behind my desk when he's around."

"Heavens! Look at the time!" said Lily, "I'd better get going on the ironing and not be back too late for Mum."

Chapter 25

GUY MORGAN, 'SUPER' archdeacon of Daneford, rang the bell of St. Olaf's Rectory. He had been asked by the bishop to try and sort out the problem in the school between Laurence Finch and Wendy.

Wendy brought him into her study. Normally, she would have brought fellow clergy into the kitchen, but she wasn't sure of Guy and decided to keep it formal—and keep her guard up—until she knew where it was all going.

She sat, waiting for him to make the first move.

"Ah, yes, well now. Super! As you know, Bishop Arthur has asked me to have a chat with you about the little problem in your school. I understand there's been a bit of a falling-out between you and the principal, Mr. Finch."

"No, I haven't fallen out with the principal. I think it may be the other way round. I'm afraid the bishop has only heard one side of the story, and when I rang him, he didn't seem to be interested to hear my side, which I find very strange. In fact, he didn't even have the courtesy, or the fairness, to inform me when Laurence Finch made the complaint. And that has happened twice." Wendy's voice was controlled, but there was no mistaking the hurt and anger she felt.

"I am only aware of the latest call from Mr. Finch. When was the other one?" Guy asked.

Wendy told the archdeacon about the spat over the Stone children and how she learned from the principal, and not from Arthur, that he had spoken to the bishop.

"Right," said Guy, refusing to offer an opinion or give any backing to Wendy. "And the present difficulty?"

Wendy filled him in on the visit from the three parents with their request for support at the AGM, her refusal, her noncommittal response at the meeting and Laurence Finch's subsequent verbal attack when she was next in school.

"Oh dear," said Guy at last. "That is not the story the bishop was given. He is of the opinion that you and one of the teachers—" he consulted his notebook "—a Miss Shilling, who is also one of your parishioners, were conspiring together to undermine Mr. Finch's authority and position in the school."

"What absolute rubbish!"

"You deny that the two of you were 'in cahoots', to use Mr. Finch's phrase? The bishop thinks Miss Shilling is a bit of a troublemaker. Mr. Finch has also contacted the bishop about her."

"Susan Shilling has only been coming to St. Olaf's recently. Apparently, she had been attending the cathedral, but then decided to come to St. Olaf's. I haven't had time to go and talk to her about her decision. But I can tell you categorically that she has not been in contact with me in any way about Laurence Finch. He has been uncooperative and distant since our board's honorary treasurer wanted to change how the accounts were managed."

Wendy went on to tell the archdeacon about Laurence's refusal to give up his own account and how he, again, accused Wendy of trying to undermine him.

"The trouble is," said Guy, "the whole situation is in danger of escalating. It appears Laurence Finch has also complained to his union, and they have been in touch with the bishop, as the patron. This could get very nasty."

"As far as I can see, the only person who has got nasty is Laurence Finch in his misinterpretation and misrepresentation of events." Wendy was not impressed.

"Perhaps you could send me a written account of those incidents," Guy suggested. "The bishop will have to know the details if the union gets stroppy and decides to take the matter further. Super! Yes! you can email it to me and I will pass it on to the bishop together with notes about our meeting today." Guy got up, and Wendy showed him to the door.

After he'd left, she sat in the kitchen, dumbfounded. No support, no sympathy, no pastoral care. Just an attempt to get authority out of a fix. It was one of those moments in ministry when she felt very isolated, hurt and vulnerable, and her bloody bishop was not helping her in any way.

Chapter 26

ANNABEL CRIED OFF the flower rota for the following Sunday, sending a message to the rota organiser that she had been struck down by a virus. She was an accomplished flower arranger and the rota was one of the few parish activities in which she took part.

She looked at her face in the mirror and saw that her cheek had turned black and blue. The swelling had nearly closed her right eye.

She was not a pretty sight. She'd have to lie low until the bruising had gone. Wouldn't the parish gossips have a field day if they got a whiff of what had happened! She wasn't popular with parishioners as she never held back on her opinions, especially if they went contrary to the tight mores of conservative Protestantism. And the women especially didn't like the flashy way she dressed, though the men had no problem there!

At the moment, she was sore, both physically and emotionally, and the fact that any man, not to mention her dull and dreary husband, would resort to physical violence revolted and disgusted her.

She sat down with a cup of coffee to plan her revenge.

Her first thought was to tell the bishop and have Anthony carpeted and humiliated. She knew that Anthony despised the bishop and thought him to be an arse. She knew how disappointed he still was not to have been made archdeacon, and how he would curl up and die inside if he had to be reprimanded—maybe even have his licence suspended—by Arthur Easterby.

Anthony must have realised that would be an option for Annabel, but she would keep him in suspense until she finally made up her mind.

There had been no communication between them since the incident, and they had gone out of their way to avoid each other. Anthony had moved into the guest bedroom and Annabel only got up when she'd heard Anthony go out in the morning. She left him meals on the kitchen table but absented herself from any contact when she heard him come into the house.

Anthony spent most of his time, when at home, in his study. Annabel spent most of her time at her daughter's house.

As it happened, Nigel was back in the Theological Institute for the November Intern Week, and this was to be followed by a reading week, so he wouldn't be around St. Aidan's for a few weeks, by which time Annabel hoped that the swelling and the bruising would be gone.

But, she was determined she would have her revenge. Her daughter told her to pack her bags and leave, and had even taken a photo of her mother's face as proof of what had happened. She was disgusted that her father would lift his hand to his wife, her mother.

In the meantime, Annabel took some pleasure in thinking how Anthony must be fearing a call from the bishop.

And what of Anthony?

He was full of anger, loathing and fear. The anger was directed at Annabel because he was convinced she was trying to lure Nigel Ashurst into an affair, rekindling the romantic feelings that had once existed between them. The loathing was directed at himself because he had lost control, something on which he had prided himself. And the fear, as Annabel had predicted, was that she would inform the bishop and he would have the humiliation of having to answer to a man he detested.

Anthony kept up a façade of normality, but inwardly he was seething, and though he had never seemed a warm character, his parishioners began to notice a new coldness and impatience in his manner. His fuse was now even shorter, and there had been a few explosions over trivial matters.

He feared every phone call. What was he to do?

Chapter 27

NIGEL ASHURST ENJOYED his monthly visits back to the Theological Institute when he and his fellow deacon interns returned for a week of seminars, study and catching up. And there was usually far more of the latter than the former!

They were never in a hurry to get to seminars or lectures as they sat around the college dining room having leisurely breakfasts and talking amongst themselves. Then, after chapel each night, a gang of them would head off to the local pub, where there was a nice little snug which generations of theological students had called The Vestry. Going to a vestry meeting as a student was not the arduous activity that many would have to endure after ordination, although for some it was more spiritual!

They swapped stories, of course, about the clergy they worked with and the pastoral incidents they had encountered, and neither lost anything in the telling.

By the time they returned to their parishes after the reading week which followed their college week, it would be the beginning of December, and Christmas would be looming. While some of the interns were getting off lightly on the liturgical front, others had been asked to preach children's sermons for Christmas morning. Well, as some of the clergy reasoned, it was no use having a dog and barking yourself!

A very useful pub-vestry meeting was held to swap ideas for Christmas Day sermons, and the minutes of that meeting were kept in detail by all concerned.

Another topic that came in for a lot of discussion was the dissertation that each student had to submit by March. Some of the students had been 'foolish virgins' and had allowed themselves to be distracted by the pastoral work they had been doing, so were unprepared for the approaching dissertation deadline even though they knew it was unlikely they would get much done over Christmas. Meanwhile, the 'wise virgins' among them had been beavering away at their dissertations and were up to date. As the Institute staff told them, it was all a matter of managing and planning their time—something they would have to learn in ministry itself.

Nigel, while he enjoyed meeting his fellow students, was looking forward to getting back to parish life. His time in the navy had taught him to be orderly and prepared, and he was well up to date with his dissertation, needing only to check and edit it in the New Year.

He really enjoyed the pastoral and liturgical life in St. Aidan's. However, he found Anthony increasingly cold and aloof, and they hadn't had any of the mentoring sessions that were laid down in the guidelines. Anthony didn't do personal, and that was OK with Nigel. He was mature enough to get on with things. He did enjoy meeting up with Annabel again and listening to her outrageous opinions on the Church.

"Annabel has picked up some kind of bug," Anthony announced to Nigel in the church vestry on his first Sunday back. "She's quite out of sorts, so I think, if you don't mind, that we will have the staff meeting here in the vestry in the morning. Oh, and it's probably best if you don't call around to the rectory.

We can't have you catching her bug in the busy run-up to Christmas. I'll let you know about the following week's meeting."

They met in the vestry the next morning, and Nigel brought along a bunch of flowers and a get well-card for Annabel, asking Anthony to pass them on to her. Anthony's only response was a "Humph!" which Nigel thought strange.

Poor Annabel, thought Nigel. *She's not getting a lot of sympathy from Anthony.*

Indeed, she wasn't.

Chapter 28

CHRISTMAS WAS COMING, but in the MacDonald household you wouldn't know. Lily's mother was deteriorating, and the decline was becoming more rapid and noticeable.

Palliative nurses came twice a day to keep her mother comfortable and ensure she wasn't in pain. At first, Lily's mother had resisted the offer of a bed in the local hospice, but accepting that she wasn't going to get better and not wanting to put more burdens on Lily, she at last relented.

As they had few friends and really only each other for company, Lily wanted to spend as much time as possible with her mother. She told the Easterbys that if she couldn't reduce her hours for the next while, she would have to give up her job in the See House.

"Christmas is not really a very busy time for bishops," Sarah had replied, much to Arthur's annoyance. He always liked to be thought of as busy. "The clergy are up to their eyes in December and don't want a bishop hanging around their parishes. Even my own office is less busy. So, yes, we do understand your situation. What about doing just two hours on two days, and we'll see how things are in the New Year?"

Lily was glad of the arrangement. Her two days a week in the See House were a distraction, and it meant she could keep in regular touch with Louise.

The staff in the hospice were great, giving as much time as was needed both to Lily and her mother. But the prognosis was bleak, and Lily's mother lapsed into a coma. She died a week later.

Neither Lily nor her mother had been church attenders. Her mother had never shown any interest in the Church and had never encouraged Lily to join either a church or any of its organisations. Technically, because of where they lived, they belonged to St. Olaf's, or so Lily supposed, as the parish magazine was dropped into her door each month. The hospice chaplain had given Lily the details of Wendy Morris, and assured Lily that she would find Wendy sympathetic and helpful.

But before she contacted Wendy, Lily wondered if her mother had left any instructions about her funeral. Whilst being close in every way, her mother had never discussed death or funerals with Lily, even in the last weeks. It had been a taboo subject. Maybe Lily would find some instructions among her personal things.

Lily went home and did something she had never done in her life—opened the drawers in her mother's dressing table. They had both respected each other's privacy. It was part of the way they lived together.

Opening the top drawer, Lily found a cardboard box on the top of which was written *FOR LILY WHEN I DIE*. In it were two savings books, which Lily immediately saw were in her name as well as her mother's. There was quite a substantial amount in both of them, and a wad of notes as well as details of an insurance policy which would pay for funeral expenses.

On a separate card entitled *FUNERAL ARRANGEMENTS*, Lily's mother had simply written:

> *I want my remains to be cremated, and I would like my ashes to be buried in my parents' grave.*

The note went on to give the details of the town and churchyard:

> *I will leave it up to you whether you want a church service or not, but my own preference would be for*

a simple private service at the crematorium. I do not
want my death to be announced in any newspapers.

At the bottom of the box was an envelope on which was written:

*TO BE OPENED **ONLY** AFTER MY FUNERAL.*

Though intrigued by what might be in it, Lily put it aside, determined to abide by her mother's wishes.

In the meantime, there were all sorts of details that had to be attended to. She would need to get in touch with funeral directors, and then she would contact Wendy Morris for a simple crematorium service.

She would have to take a few days off and rang the See House to tell them her mother had passed away and she wouldn't be in until after Christmas. Arthur offered her his sympathy and any help she might need. He asked for details about when the service might be and said he would attend. But Lily said there was no need as her mother had requested a private ceremony.

Chapter 29

As Christmas approached, the temperature dropped and the papers were predicting a white Christmas.

Whatever the weather outside, the temperature was decidedly glacial inside St. Aidan's Rectory. Although they were living under one roof, Anthony and Annabel managed to avoid each other completely.

The bruising on Annabel's face was clearing and she was able to disguise it with make-up, but the emotional bruising had not diminished and she was still sore inside.

Of course, Annabel hadn't seen Nigel for weeks, and she had missed his company. She decided that she would call around now that he was back from his intern and reading weeks. She would bring a little Christmas gift as an excuse for calling. She had seen a rather smart tie while out shopping and could imagine Nigel wearing it.

Nigel's Mazda MX5 was in the driveway as she drove up, so he was certain to be at home.

"Annabel, what a pleasant surprise! Anthony told me how poorly you were. I hope you are feeling better—you are certainly looking well. Come in and have a cup of coffee, if you have the time."

"Yes, I am feeling a lot better, thank you, and yes, I have time for coffee."

Nigel led the way into the kitchen and switched on the coffee machine.

"I'm sure Anthony must be up to his eyes with work. I was sorry to have been away for the last two weeks, but we had our meeting this morning, and he's given me a long list to make up for the time away. From what I hear, you had a pretty nasty bout."

"Well, yes, it was. It completely knocked me off my feet. But hey-ho! I've bounced back. I've brought you a little something for Christmas. I know it's a bit early, but when I saw it, I thought of you." She handed him the gift-wrapped tie.

"Oh, you really shouldn't have!" Nigel replied, embarrassed. "I'm afraid all I have for you and Anthony are two bottles of wine!" He unwrapped the present. "But this is very dashing. Thank you so much! I'll wear it to a few parties I'm going to over Christmas, and it will sure be good for my image!"

He went over to Annabel and kissed her lightly on the cheek.

Annabel's heart fluttered, and while she would have liked to reciprocate, she also didn't want to rush things with Nigel. He was only two years widowed, and she knew from their conversations that his had been a very happy marriage.

Annabel listened with one ear to Nigel's stories about his fellow ordinands and the various happenings during their intern week. The other half of her mind was thinking what a good relationship she could have with Nigel, how compatible they were, and what might happen if Anthony wasn't around.

She knew she was entering the world of fantasy, but she was rather enjoying it. As she looked admiringly at Nigel, she wondered whether she could have more than revenge on Anthony.

"I'm afraid I have to go to the school now. They are preparing the carol service and I've been drafted in to help." Nigel took the cup out of Annabel's hand, breaking her out of her reverie.

"Oh, sorry, I just drifted there a bit! Must be the after-effect of the virus," Annabel apologised as she got up to go. "It's so good to see you again, Nigel. I'll keep in touch."

As she drove home to the rectory, she finally made up her mind. She would tell the bishop about Anthony's assault. She would disgrace him and free herself of him. Nigel was sure to take her side and take pity on her. Who knew what it might lead to?

She was getting further and further into fantasy land, blind to all the practicalities of a clerical marriage break-up, not to mention the public gossip and rumour mill that accompanied such events. She was an impulsive teenager again and was thoroughly enjoying it.

Arriving back at the rectory, without even taking her coat off, she picked up the phone and dialled the See House.

Chapter 30

WENDY MORRIS, RECTOR of St. Olaf's, like all clergy, felt the pressure of the weeks leading up to Christmas. There were special services to prepare, extra readers to be arranged, a list of private communions to the housebound to be got through, civic carol singing, charity carol singing and, of course, the school carol service which was held in the church each year so that daddies and mammies, grandads and grandmas, and recent past pupils could come and see the children singing, reading or playing an instrument.

It was really a concert more than a service, as proud parents stood on pews with their phones to get photos or record a video. Wendy didn't mind. It was good PR for the parish and a chance to say hello to parents and friends. While the school organised the service, Wendy arranged for microphones to be placed where they were needed and a screen to be ready for the accompanying PowerPoint. She also needed to check on what she was being asked to do in the service, as there was no one as tetchy as Laurence Finch if anything went wrong on such a public occasion.

Usually, Wendy would just drop into the school, but in light of all that had happened recently, she felt it would be more appropriate—and safer—to make an appointment with the principal through the school secretary.

So Wendy arrived at St. Olaf's school and was shown in to the principal's office. Laurence Finch had company. A man with a folder in front of him was sitting beside Laurence's desk. Not knowing the man, Wendy started to leave the room, thinking that Laurence was still in a meeting.

"No, Reverend Morris, please come in," said Laurence.

Looking at the man seated with him, Wendy said, "It's OK, I'll wait outside until you're ready."

"Ah," said Laurence, a tic throbbing in his temple, "we are ready."

Wendy frowned and looked towards the man with the folder.

"This is Mr. Taggart. He's an official from our teachers' union, and I have requested his presence at all the meetings between me and you in the light of how you have schemed with others to undermine my position as principal."

Mr. Taggart looked uncomfortable, the picture of a person who did not want to be drawn into such a petty dispute.

Wendy was taken aback. "Why was I not informed of this development? Surely it would have been good manners and courtesy to have let me know?"

"I did, of course, inform the bishop as patron," replied Laurence. "I'm afraid that I can't be held responsible for a breakdown in the internal communications of the Church." He smiled bleakly. "Now, can we please get down to business about the carol service. We don't need to talk about board of management business today, as there won't be another meeting until late January. Do take a seat, Reverend Morris." He indicated a chair opposite his desk.

The meeting was short, but it was a huge waste of time for the union official, and as Wendy drove back to the rectory, her blood was boiling. Why had the bishop not informed her of this latest development? Why did he even agree to it? Again, she felt humiliated and undermined. Bloody Bishop! Had he lost all sense of loyalty and pastoral care? Didn't he care for his hard-working clergy? She immediately rang the See House. The bishop wasn't in, so his secretary, Louise, got an earful.

"Gosh, Wendy, I'm really sorry you weren't told. I saw the letter that came in from Laurence Finch and the union. I know that the bishop passed it on to the archdeacon, as he had already talked to you about the school. He asked Guy to let you know."

"Well, he didn't, and at the moment I feel like a piece of…dog poo that those in authority seem to be avoiding in case they get some on their precious ecclesiastical shoes."

She put the phone down and rang Guy.

"Oh, Hi, Wendy! Super! You know, you must be psychic. I was just about to ring you, eh, about a little matter in connection with the school."

"Well, you're too late!" Wendy's voice was taut. "I've just been to the school to be confronted with a union official sitting beside the principal. I could have done with a bit of advance knowledge about it. It is no 'little matter', as you choose to describe it. I was made to look stupid, and I've been humiliated. What is it with you and the bishop? Don't either of you care?"

"Oh, Wendy, I'm so sorry. But you know what Christmas is like in the parish with so much going on. I know I should have rung you earlier, but I didn't think a meeting in the school was imminent. Again, I'm really sorry. Why don't you put the kettle on and I'll drop round now for a cup of coffee and a chat?"

"Don't bother. I'm sure you've got a hundred and one more important things to do," Wendy replied coldly and put down the phone.

There were tears in her eyes. *You work your guts out. You put up with the flak. You smile and be friendly towards those you know are criticising you behind your back. You do your best and then the institution lets you down!*

She had just sat down for a cup of coffee and some comfort food when the doorbell rang.

She looked at her watch. "Oh, shit! I forgot someone called Lily MacDonald was coming to talk about a funeral." She splashed her face with water, straightened herself up, put on a smile and went to the front door.

Chapter 31

THE PHONE CALL that Anthony was dreading came at last. Though it wasn't from the bishop but from Super Guy, the archdeacon, whom he equally detested.

"Oh, hi, Anthony. This is Guy Morgan here. I wonder if we could have a chat sometime soon. It's a bit of a delicate matter, so I'm wondering if you could come over to my rectory. I know that we'll be private here. Listen, I'm free for the early part of the afternoon, so let's say two o'clock."

It sounded to Anthony more like a command than a request. He was in no position to argue, so he just said, "OK," and hung up. He buried his face in his hands. "Oh God, what a mess. What a stupid, bloody mess!"

In a way he was relieved. He knew that Annabel, at least in her present frame of mind, was likely to tell the bishop. She would see it as sweet revenge. For the last few weeks, he had lived with the prospect of being hauled before the bishop, and he was a nervous wreck.

What had cracked his self-control to hit Annabel? It was so out of character. But the way she was flirting with Nigel had become intolerable to him. Anthony and Annabel had never enjoyed a close relationship, which he regretted now. They had just drifted apart. She wasn't interested in the Church, and he wasn't interested in what she did. Maybe he should have made more of an effort—years ago—but somehow he'd let parish work suck up more and more of his time. A bit like that experiment of the frog in the water in which the temperature kept getting hotter and it didn't seem to notice. He remembered someone once describing the job of a cleric as 'the doughnut with the hole on the outside'—there was no end to what a dedicated cleric might do. There were no real boundaries, no real job description. The Church could soak up all your time and energy, and still there was more that could be done. He was of the generation of ordinands who had imbibed the mantra 'First the Church, then God and lastly your family'.

He had heard from Nigel that new clergy were taught to reverse that order. But it was too late for him. The damage had been done.

"Oh God, Oh God!" Tears ran down his cheeks. What an end—for he was sure of that—to his ministry. He had longed for promotion to archdeacon. Now all that faced him was disgrace.

***

They sat in Guy's study.

"Bishop Arthur had a phone call from your wife, Annabel. She claims that you were physically violent towards her. In fact, that you hit her and knocked her to the floor. The bishop has asked me to hear your side of the story."

"Well, yes. As much as it pains me to admit it, I did strike out at Annabel and she fell down as a result." Anthony avoided eye contact with the archdeacon.

"But Anthony, this is not at all like you. You always seem so in charge of your feelings. What prompted you to do such a thing?"

"I let myself be provoked by Annabel, and I started to imagine a situation that was far from reality."

"Like what?" prompted Guy.

'Well, you see, my deacon intern, the one you asked me to take, Nigel Ashurst, was at school with Annabel. I understand that they were boyfriend and girlfriend in their last year. Of course, they both went their separate ways when they left school and the relationship ended. Nigel married and joined the navy, and Annabel and I met and were married. It's just…she seemed to enjoy flirting with Nigel when they met again, and I found it… both irritating and childish, to the extreme."

"And Nigel, what about him? Did he lead her on in this flirtation?"

"No! I must make it perfectly clear on this. I don't think Nigel really noticed what Annabel was up to. His behaviour has been entirely proper, and I've no complaint there. It's Annabel who's been doing the running, knowing it would annoy me and make me feel jealous and, I suppose, inadequate. On the day I hit her, she had taunted me beyond endurance, and I'm sorry to say I snapped."

"This is quite a serious matter," said Guy. "Especially as Annabel has made a formal complaint. I'll talk about it to the bishop. Maybe we'll have to take some legal advice." He paused, then added, "We could be looking at some disciplinary consequences, maybe even suspension."

Anthony, for the second time that day, buried his head in his hands. "God, what a bloody mess I've made, and what a way to end my ministry!"

"Let's not assume anything," said Guy. "What if Annabel withdrew her complaint? Do you think she could be persuaded?"

"I don't know what to think," replied Anthony. "I don't know what's got into her this last while. We were never what you might call 'lovey-dovey', but we got on in our own way. Now it's all turned upside down. I just don't know any longer."

Guy couldn't wish Anthony a 'Happy Christmas' as they walked to the door, but he had to say something. "Look, old chap, I'll be thinking of you at this difficult time," he said weakly.

Anthony, a broken man, walked stiffly to his car.

Chapter 32

LILY WAS DETERMINED to abide by her mother's wishes and to have just a simple, private service at the crematorium. That was what she asked Wendy Morris to take when she called to see her. Little did Lily know of all that Wendy had already endured that morning. To Lily, she was calm, collected and sympathetic.

"As you know, my mother was not a church attender," explained Lily. "She seemed quite bitter about the church but would never discuss it with me. However, I do know that she believed in God and did pray."

"Well, none of us can judge anyone else. That's not our job. I'm here to help and do what I can."

They decided not to have any hymns. In any case, there would be few to sing, probably just her friend Louise and a few distant relatives. It was all to be very low key.

"Mum wanted her ashes to be buried in her parents' grave down the country. But I can contact the local rector to do that sometime in the spring."

Wendy was relieved. Her diary for Christmas was full. A simple crematorium service could be fitted in, whereas a full church service would have put a great deal of pressure on her time.

Two days later, a small group of people gathered at the crematorium to say goodbye to Lily's mother. Bishop Arthur slipped into the back row. Both he and Sarah appreciated Lily's quiet efficiency in the See House, and he had found out from his secretary Louise when and where the funeral would be held so he could pay his respects. He shook Lily's hand at the end of the service and left immediately. Both he and Wendy made sure to avoid each other.

Lily and her few relatives returned to their flat where Louise had helped Lily prepare some refreshments. The relatives were anxious to be on the road before dark and left soon afterwards.

When everything had been cleared away, Lily and Louise sat down for a drink and a chat. By seven p.m., Louise had left and Lily was alone. She didn't fancy looking at television which, around Christmas, was going to be full of jolly festive programmes, which seemed inappropriate on the night of her mother's funeral. So she sat quietly in front of the fire, a glass of wine in her hand, her mind full of memories of growing up—of her and her mother, as her memories of her father were vague. A few trips to the seaside and to the cinema. She remembered nothing of him as a person, and if it wasn't for the photographs around the house, she wouldn't have been able to describe him in any detail, except that he seemed to be much older than her mother. But she did recall that he was kind, and that their home was a happy one.

She let her mind drift through a kaleidoscope of holidays she and her mother had taken, and she smiled at how sometimes they were taken as sisters rather than mother and daughter. Her mother was pleased when that happened, though Lily never regarded it as a compliment to herself!

She was grateful for the sincere and sensitive way that Wendy had conducted the service, and made a mental note to write a thank-you letter.

And then she remembered. That envelope her mother had left with instructions it should only be opened after her funeral.

She went to her mother's room, found the letter in the dressing table and brought it back to her chair by the fire. She poured herself another glass of wine and sat down to read it.

Dearest Lily,

It has meant so much to me to have you as a daughter and also as a friend, and I love you dearly. Although you probably don't realise it, you have made my life worthwhile. It could have been otherwise.

I never really talked much about the past to you, and I have thought long and hard about whether to tell you what I am about to write. In one way, you would be better off not knowing, but in another way, I feel I owe it to you.

The fact is…

Lily couldn't believe what she was reading. She read and re-read the letter. Her mind was in a spin. She poured herself another drink.

Chapter 33

ARCHDEACON GUY WAS in Arthur's study, discussing Anthony Parker's situation.

"I think you really ought to have a word with him," said Guy. "But go gently with him. He is a very broken man."

"He's also a very annoying man," retorted Arthur. "I can imagine him at council meetings criticising me to his neighbours. That man has an inflated sense of his own importance."

"Well, he is a very deflated man at the moment."

"I'll have to get some legal advice on this," Arthur went on, "but I won't be able to contact anyone now until after the holiday period. As you know, Sarah and I are going away for a few days after Christmas. We're thinking of buying a cottage, and we're off to do some scouting around to see what's on the market. But—" there was a vengeful glint in the bishop's eye "—I think I'll have a word with him, just the same. Keep the pressure on him."

Having seen what a broken man Anthony had become, Guy had more sympathy for him than the bishop had.

"Of course," Guy said, "it might throw a different light on it if Annabel withdrew her complaint. I did mention that possibility to Anthony, though he seemed to think it was unlikely."

Guy was not a full-time archdeacon and was rather pressed for time. He had a lot of parochial matters to attend to and couldn't hang around, so he said his goodbyes and left.

Arthur, by contrast, had not much to attend to. Christmas was a bit of a lull time for bishops. Meetings had stopped. Clergy were at full tilt, and Arthur had only a Christmas sermon to write for the cathedral. Yes, the more he thought about it, the more he liked the idea of making Anthony squirm a bit. He took up the phone, got Anthony and arranged for him to come to the See House later that afternoon.

He fiddled with his pectoral cross, switched on his computer and started thinking about his Christmas sermon.

***

The bishop had caught Anthony as he was leaving the house for a meeting with Nigel Ashurst in the church vestry. They were due to finalise the arrangements for Christmas and after.

Nigel was waiting in the church when Anthony came in shaking slightly with beads of perspiration on his forehead.

"My word, Anthony, you don't look at all well. I hope you're not coming down with flu. That's the last thing you want at this time of year." Nigel was concerned at Anthony's appearance.

Anthony slumped into a chair and mopped his brow. The handkerchief looked rumpled and well used, not the usual freshly laundered one he always seemed to have. "The flu would be preferable," he mumbled.

"Sorry, I didn't catch what you said."

"Oh, nothing." Anthony tried to pass it off. At this moment, he was at his lowest ebb—what, after having a meeting with an archdeacon whom he disliked and now facing a meeting with a bishop he detested—but he had brought all this trouble on himself.

"Don't you think you should go home and keep warm, see if you can shake off whatever it is?" Nigel suggested.

"That's the last place I want to be!" said Anthony feebly. He could see the look of puzzlement on Nigel's face. It was all going to come out eventually, and Nigel's name was going to be connected with the mess, however much an innocent party he might be. Nothing ever remained confidential in the Church, and in spite of Annabel's infatuation, Anthony liked and respected Nigel, so it was only fair he should tell him what had happened and why.

"First, let's go over the Christmas arrangements, and then we need to have a chat, as I'm afraid it's not the flu that has me in this state."

Nigel was perplexed but knew he would just have to wait.

They got themselves sorted over who was doing what at the various Christmas services. Before they started looking at the Sundays after Christmas, Anthony, without meeting Nigel's eyes, said, "The thing is, I don't know whether I'll be here after Christmas."

Nigel started to ask why, but Anthony shushed him. "This is going to be very awkward and embarrassing."

***

When Anthony had finished, it was Nigel's turn to mop his brow. "I had no idea this was all going on. I thought Annabel was just being...well, Annabel. She was always a bit gushing even when we were at school. She could turn on the charm to anyone and make them feel they were special to her, even if they weren't. So I'm afraid a lot of what she said and did just washed over me. I wouldn't for the world have encouraged her, in any way, to be disloyal or unfaithful to you. As you say, what a horrible mess!"

"And I'm old enough to have had more sense," Anthony said. "I know what Annabel is like, how flighty she can be. I admit I had let our relationship drift and not given her much time and attention. But when I saw how attentive she was to you, and how bubbly she became when you were around, I suppose...well, if I'm honest...I became jealous, and stupidly, I let it get to me. It started to eat at me, and I began to imagine situations that weren't there. But—" Anthony looked straight at Nigel "—I have told the archdeacon, and I will tell the bishop, categorically, that you are an innocent party and in no way encouraged Annabel."

"What will happen?' asked Nigel as the consequences began to sink in.

'I don't really know," replied Anthony. "The archdeacon did hint at some disciplinary process, but I reckon I am finished here in St. Aidan's."

Nigel had never felt so helpless as he noticed a tear roll its way down Anthony's cheek.

Chapter 34

I KNOW IT'S SHORT notice, but is there any chance you could come round to my house for lunch?" Nigel asked Annabel on the phone.

"Oh, what a lovely surprise! Of course! I look forward to it!" Annabel was her bright and breezy self. "And I'll bring something sweet for dessert. See you soon!"

Annabel was surprised to see Nigel dressed formally in his collar, but supposed that he was coming and going to visits all day. She was also surprised, and disappointed, when he didn't kiss her proffered cheek. *Oh, well*, she thought, *clergy get harried and hassled at this time of year.* She would put him at ease and make him relax, make him appreciate her company and show him how things in the future might be.

"I'm sorry it's all ready-made," said Nigel, taking two containers out of the oven. "It was all a bit last-minute."

"I do like spontaneity," beamed Annabel. "It's so romantic!" She laid her hand on Nigel's arm.

Nigel motioned to Annabel to have a seat.

"Before you sit down, get two glasses. I've brought round a rather good wine that you'll like." Annabel produced an expensive-looking bottle from her bag.

"I've a lot on this afternoon, so I'd better not have anything alcoholic to drink," Nigel demurred. "And anyway, we need to have a serious chat."

Annabel's mind began to race. Was Nigel beginning to feel the same way about her as she did about him? Was she right all along that he was still attracted to her? Were her dreams more real than fantasies?

She looked at him coyly. She sensed that he was having difficulty over what to say. She waited.

"Look, we've always got on well together," he began, his eyes focused on the plate in front of him, while hers were bright with anticipation.

"Yes, yes, we have!" she agreed.

"But a lot of things have happened since our time in school. We got married to different people. My wife, unfortunately, died, but your husband is still alive."

"Yes, I know I'm not free," said Annabel. "But one day, soon, I promise—"

"You just don't get it, do you, Annabel?" Nigel's voice was harsh. "There's nothing romantic between us, and there never will be. You've been fantasising and letting it interfere with your relationship with Anthony."

"There never was much of a relationship there. It soon went cold," sniffed Annabel. "Not like the relationship we had together—and could still have!"

"Annabel, please listen to me! Anthony has told me everything—yes, everything! You're about to wreck his career, having wrecked him as a person already."

"No more than he has done to my life. He deserves it. And did he tell you that he assaulted me and threw me to the ground? That I nursed a black eye for weeks, and that is why staff meetings couldn't be held in the rectory—in case you saw what he did to me. You don't know what a brute he has become!"

"Annabel, I will not come between you and Anthony. But I do plead with you to do one thing. Please withdraw your complaint to the bishop. Put an end to this nonsense and let both of you get your lives back."

Tears came streaming down Annabel's cheeks. "First, Anthony turns on me. And now you, of all people!" She pushed her plate away. "I'm not hungry. I must be going. This is not the kind of lunch I thought I would be having."

"I'm sorry, Annabel, if you got the wrong end of the stick. But please, I beg you, don't go through with this. There are no winners, only losers, at the end of the day. Please make it up with Anthony. Talk to the bishop before it's too late."

He stayed sitting at the table as she rushed out of the house, wailing loudly.

***

Just as he was leaving to go to the See House, Anthony received a call from the bishop.

"There's no need to come to see me this afternoon," said Arthur. "Annabel has just phoned and has withdrawn her complaint. I hope this will be a warning to you." And he rang off.

Anthony flooded with relief. Yes, it would, after all, be a happier Christmas than he thought he would have had.

Chapter 35

THE REVD. WENDY Morris was putting away microphones and platforms after the school service. Parents and children had left in high spirits, as had the teachers who were going to a local pub to have Christmas drinks with the principal, Laurence Finch. It was the same every year.

"Is there anything I can do to help?" came a voice from behind Wendy. When she turned around, she saw Susan Shilling standing there.

"Are you not off to Christmas drinks with the others?" asked Wendy.

"No, I'm going to give that a miss." Susan paused. "You may know that I am not the flavour of the month with Mr. Finch."

"Well, that makes two of us!" responded Wendy. "What happened to you?"

"It all started when I approached Mr. Finch about taking in the Stone children. Their mother comes from the same town as I do. In fact, we were in school together, and she asked me to put in a good word for the two boys."

"Oh dear, that was not a pleasant one," recalled Wendy. "I'm afraid that didn't help my relationship with Laurence Finch either."

"Actually, the principal accused me of being in cahoots with you over the matter, and ever since he has frozen me out and made life in the school as difficult as possible for me."

"Yes, that seems to be the way Laurence Finch works. Once you disagree or upset him, a line is crossed, and from then on you are always on the opposite side. Did you ever think of moving to another school? Make a fresh start?"

"The problem is that there are very few vacancies around. Only temporary positions, and I have a mortgage to pay, so that's not really an option at the moment. My boyfriend has moved in, and he is helping with the repayments."

There was silence for a few moments, and then Susan continued, "Actually, I did think of being ordained. I was attending the cathedral before I started coming here. They were very supportive and so was Peter Pearce, the DDO, but I'm afraid I wasn't recommended."

"That's hard to understand," said Wendy. "With your experience as a teacher and with the support of the DDO and cathedral clergy, that should have been enough to get you recommended for training."

"I don't think Bishop Easterby was too keen on me. My interview with him didn't go well. He didn't give me any sense that he was supportive—he was very offhand and cool. I can't help wondering if Laurence Finch didn't put in a complaint about me to the bishop, making me out to be a troublemaker, and that affected the outcome. Anyway—" Susan smiled and put on a brave face, "—that is all in the past. Peter Pearce did suggest trying again in two years, but if the bishop isn't behind me, it would all be a waste of time. It was hurtful enough as it was!"

"That's an awful pity." Wendy readily realised what had happened. After all, Laurence Finch had reported her to the bishop as well. But she kept her counsel.

"I've started training with the Samaritans, and I'm really enjoying that," Susan said, and they continued to chat as they put away the equipment and rearranged the front of the church. "I suppose you'll have a busy Christmas, what with all the services. What do you do when they're all finished?"

"I collapse on to the sofa and then make something to eat!" Wendy replied. "Well, I don't actually make anything. I have just enough energy to pop something from Marks and Sparks into the oven. I could go to friends', but by then I've had enough, so I put my feet up and watch—or maybe fall asleep in front of—the telly! What about you? Do you go home?"

"My mother died just over a year ago, and my sister is having Dad over for the day, so Robbie—that's my boyfriend—and I are going to stay in Lislea. I'll go and see my family on Stephen's Day, and Robbie will go to his family. We're not planning to be eating until late afternoon." Susan hesitated. "Why don't you come round and join us? I'm afraid I have bought in too much for the two of us. You'd be doing us a favour, actually, as we're both going away the next day, and the food will be only going to waste. I'd like you to meet Robbie. After all, we might have a job for you to do in the not too distant future! And you can go home whenever you like. We won't be offended!"

With all the hassle that Wendy had had recently, Christmas was going to be a rather glum affair after all the services had finished. She had enjoyed talking to Susan and getting to know her. *What the hell!* she thought. *It can't be any worse than being on my own.*

"Do you know, I'd be delighted to accept your invitation! I'll bring the wine!"

Chapter 36

Anthony sat at his desk, trying to write a Christmas sermon. It was getting late and only his desk lamp was on, leaving the rest of his study in semi-darkness.

What new slant could he put on the Christmas message? Nigel was preaching on Christmas morning, thank goodness. That sermon would have to appeal to adults and children and those who only came at Christmas. Not an easy one to prepare! Anthony was going to preach at the midnight communion. Up to today, he couldn't even bring himself to think about a sermon, but with the cancellation of the interview with the bishop, and Annabel's withdrawal of her complaint, a new shaft of light and hope shone, lifting his gloom-laden heart enough to begin to think of an address.

He'd gathered a pile of books and commentaries on his desk, seeking inspiration, and at long last, he was concentrating on something other than his bleak future. The door creaked slightly. He just about heard it and swivelled his chair around. He mustn't have closed it properly. But then he saw the handle move and a hand appear around the door.

A female hand. Annabel's hand!

She appeared in the doorway, silhouetted by the hall light.

"Anthony, I need to talk to you."

She came into the study. Even in the gloom he could see that she had none of the poise and confidence she usually had.

"I've come to a decision," she said. "After all that has happened between us, I think it best if I leave. I have my bags packed and I will go first thing tomorrow. I've arranged to go to Lucy and Chris initially, and then in the New Year, I'll look to see what's available—far away from Lislea."

Anthony had his back to the desk so his face was in shadow. Annabel couldn't read his expression, but he could see her eyes were red and her cheeks glistened from crying. He didn't know what to say.

Before he could say anything, Annabel continued, "We have both been unbelievably stupid. I don't know what got into the two of us. But whatever there was between the two of us has gone. It's over!"

Anthony cleared his throat to speak, but Annabel held up her hand. "There was no affair between me and Nigel. Nigel has been completely honourable and completely loyal to you. Yes, perhaps I flaunted myself at him, knowing how much it would annoy you. I got pleasure in that! I suppose I even thought I could rekindle what was, after all, only a teenage romance. And I know how I have hurt you and jeopardised your career. For that, I'm sorry. But you also…" She paused. "Let's just say that with all that's happened, I don't see a future together."

The silence hung between them. Anthony's face was still in dark shadow.

She started to leave, but Anthony quickly got up and went over to her. The light caught his face, and she saw there were tears in his eyes.

"We were both at fault. I, as much as you. And what I did, in hitting you, was unforgivable, totally unforgivable. I am so, so sorry. I should not have done that. I realised it as soon as I did it."

He put up his hand. "Now let me speak." He waited for her to sit down then perched on the arm of her chair. "I know things haven't been great between us for a number of years, and I did little to improve the situation. I paid more attention to the Church than to you, and soon it became a way of life.

Climbing up the greasy pole of preferment was all I thought about, and look what it has done to me—and to our marriage!"

He paused, and then looked at her. "I know that I am not—and have never been, truth to tell—the most exciting of husbands but..." His voice began to crack. "...although you may not have seen much evidence of it, I do love you, deeply and sincerely. I only realised how much when I thought I had lost you."

He put his arm around her shoulders, expecting it to be pushed away, but she reached up and took his hand in hers. They were both silent for a few moments.

In a soft voice, Annabel said, "What a terrible mess we've made! But where do we go from here?"

"Perhaps it's time for a new start, for both of us, in a new place. I've been here in St. Aidan's for fifteen years now. It's probably time I moved on. Let's make a complete break and move to another diocese—to another part of the country altogether. Maybe even a less busy parish. Let's see if we can both make a fresh go of our lives."

Chapter 37

THE SEE HOUSE was in a post-Christmas mess, and Sarah Easterby was in no mood to start clearing it up. There were piles of dishes to be done, wrappers and pieces of Christmas paper everywhere. Their children and grandchildren had left to go to the in-laws for the New Year, and their detritus was all over the place.

Arthur had promised Sarah that after Christmas they would take a few days off. They had decided they would try to buy a holiday cottage in the south or west and had googled a few possibilities to look at on their break.

Arthur was going to take his car to Robbie Taylor's garage. A warning light had appeared on the dashboard and he didn't want to set off and find out it was something serious. He promised Sarah he wouldn't be long, and he was sure they could get going by mid-morning.

"I'm too tired to start cleaning the house now," she said. "But I don't want to come back to a mess. I know what I'll do. I'll give Lily a ring and explain that we're going away for a few days, and maybe she could come around and give the house a good clean and deal with all the washing that needs doing. She did say that she would be back to us after Christmas. She can't be too busy now, what with her mother gone."

Arthur left for the garage, and Sarah rang Lily. As it happened, Lily was just about to ring Sarah. She had planned to return to work that morning, so she would be over within the hour.

"That would be absolutely marvellous," Sarah chirped, her mood improving by the minute. "I'll sort out the washing and begin to pack our case. We want to get going as soon as possible."

When Lily arrived, she realised why she was needed that morning.

Sarah was fussing around, anxious to get away as soon as Arthur returned. "We're heading first to the southwest," she told Lily. "It's hard to know what the traffic will be like this time of the year, and I'd like to get down there before it's dark so we can get our bearings."

"If it helps," Lily offered, "I can put together a picnic for you. It would save time instead of going to a restaurant for lunch."

"That's so sweet and thoughtful of you," smiled Sarah. "You'll find all you need, I think, in the fridge, and do have some of what's there for your lunch. It will hardly keep until we get back. Thank you so much!"

While Sarah went off to finish packing, Lily busied herself making sandwiches and filled a large flask with coffee; she had it all ready when Arthur came back.

"Robbie thinks it's just a faulty sensor. He gave the car a good look over, spent a bit of time checking brakes and oil levels, so I reckon we are ready to go."

"Lily has even made us a picnic," cooed Sarah, handing the basket to Arthur. "Isn't that sweet of her?"

And so it was that the Easterbys headed off in good spirits for a few days' break, leaving the mess in the house for Lily to sort out.

They headed first for Galway; Arthur got a bit delayed with local traffic but made good time on the motorway. Around lunchtime, he drew into a lay-by for their picnic.

"This is so good of Lily," Arthur said. "It will save us quite a bit of time. We will probably get to the first cottage in daylight."

They finished off their sandwiches and coffee and then resumed their journey.

The miles sped by. Arthur yawned. "Driving on motorways is so monotonous. I thought that coffee would have woken me up."

"Yes, I'm feeling a bit sleepy too," said Sarah. "I'd say Christmas is catching up with us both. Having the children and the grandchildren all over Christmas probably took more out of us than usual. Those kids never stop! Do you mind if I have a little doze? I'm afraid that I'm not up to making much conversation. Are you OK?"

"Sure, I'm fine. I'll put the radio on and lower the temperature. I hope it's not a sign that we're getting old!"

He glanced over at Sarah, who was already asleep, her head against the passenger window.

Very soon, Arthur was battling to keep his eyes open. He shifted on his seat and opened his window to let in some fresh air. He didn't want to wake Sarah and ask her to take over the wheel. Anyway, she looked to be in a deep sleep. He knew that he should pull over and have a quick snooze, but he did want to get to the first cottage they were going to look at before dark, so he drove determinedly on.

But he was fighting a losing battle. Tiredness flowed over him in waves. His eyelids felt increasingly heavy. He had left the motorway before reaching Galway and decided that at the first convenient spot he would pull over and have a quick nap, or at least a walk in the fresh air, and then finish off the coffee left in the flask.

Towns and villages became a bit of a blur, and his eyes were actually closed as he approached a major junction. He didn't see the 'stop' sign and the white markings across his side of the road. He drove straight on, right into the path of an articulated lorry whose driver had no chance of braking. The Easterbys' car was pushed into the path of traffic coming the opposite direction and it became a yo-yo until it came to a stop squashed between cars and lorries.

Drivers whipped out their mobiles to ring the emergency services. Steam and oil and glass carpeted the road, as those who were able got out of their cars, shocked and stunned. Soon the sound of sirens could be heard as ambulances and a fire engine sped to the scene of mangled vehicles.

As the paramedics made their way through the crashed cars, they found that, luckily, most of the injuries appeared relatively minor and not life-threatening. However, when they got to the Easterbys' car, or what was left of it, it was immediately evident that they had both been killed instantly.

Chapter 38

THE SEE HOUSE was empty when the police drove up to the front door and knocked. Looking at the diocesan website, the police saw that Louise Roberts was the bishop's secretary, and so it was Louise who first heard of the Easterbys' fatal accident, as the police asked for the numbers and addresses of their children.

The evening news simply reported that two people had been killed in a road accident in Co. Galway, but when the names were released the following morning, there was a widespread sense of shock not only in Daneford diocese but throughout the whole Church of Ireland.

The Church of Ireland is a small church. Everyone knows everyone else. In See Houses, deaneries and rectories up and down the country, the news was received with sadness, however much they may have criticised or been jealous of Arthur and Sarah.

***

In St. Patrick's Rectory, in the post-Christmas lull, Steve Adams was in his dressing gown, making breakfast for himself and Fiona when he heard the news on the radio. Leaving the breakfast preparations, he rushed up the stairs. "You'll never guess what's happened!" he blurted to Fiona, who was getting comfortable to have a nice lie-in, still on her Christmas break.

"No idea, you'd better tell me," she mumbled sleepily.

"Arthur Easterby! You know the bishop who stymied my appointment to St. Saviour's? Well, he has been killed in a car crash, along with his wife."

Fiona sat up. "Oh my gosh! I know he's not at the top of our favourites' list, but that's awful. Here, pass me my iPad. I'll see if there are any details."

***

Harry White, the nominator of St. Saviour's who had approached Steve Adams during their vacancy, was putting his golf clubs in his car to go off for a game with his friends. His wife called him from the front door.

"I think you'd better hear the news before you go. There's been an awful accident near Galway, and the bishop and his wife are both dead. Look, it's all in here." She opened the paper, which Harry hadn't had time to look at.

Harry went into the kitchen and spread the paper on the table. "I was never a fan of his, especially over the way he treated us over the appointment to St. Saviour's, but you've got to feel sad for their family. The poor bugger!"

"And Mrs. Easterby!" Harry's wife reminded him.

***

Susan Shilling and Robbie were driving back from seeing relatives. They had announced their engagement on Christmas Day, in the company of Wendy Morris, and were doing the rounds of families and friends to celebrate. The news on the hour came up as they listened to the radio; Susan couldn't believe her ears when she heard of the Easterbys' accident.

"And you were talking to him only yesterday morning!" Susan said to Robbie. "Didn't you say he was worried about something in his car?"

"Yes, there was an emissions light that wouldn't go out. It sometimes happens, and it's usually either an electrical or a sensor failure. It's not critical or dangerous, so he decided to wait until the main garages were open again to have it replaced. He asked me to give the car a quick check as he was off to the West. Everything seemed OK. I hope it wasn't a mechanical fault that caused the accident or they'll be accusing me, especially after the way he treated you."

Susan laughed, and then became serious. "You wouldn't have done anything, would you? I mean…"

"Can't say I wasn't tempted! He wasn't the most friendly, even though I was doing him a favour opening up the garage during the holiday period. Always seemed so superior! But no! I didn't tamper with anything, or cut the brake pipes or anything like that! Is that what you think I'm capable of doing?"

"No, of course not! But you know, with him gone, I just might think of ordination again. But not until after our wedding." Susan leaned over to kiss Robbie on the cheek.

Robbie laughed. "You'd better pay attention to the road, or you'll have us ending up like the Easterbys!"

***

Louise Roberts had rung Lily as soon as the police had left, but there was no answer. The phone just rang out. She rang again the next morning, but the phone went dead. It was Lily's mobile number, and it was very strange that there was no reply.

She got into her car and drove round to the flat where Lily had lived with her mother. Lily's car was in the drive, but there was no answer to her constant ringing of the bell.

She peered through the letterbox and looked through all the windows. The curtains weren't pulled over, and Louise could see into all the rooms. Everywhere was neat and tidy, but there was no sign of Lily.

It was not like Lily to be out of contact. Not wanting to raise a false alarm, Louise returned to her car and decided to call again at lunchtime. Lily didn't have any other real friends, but as her car was there, she was hardly working at the See House. Just to make sure, Louise made her way round to check.

Again, she drew a blank.

Chapter 39

W HAT A DREADFUL accident!" the archbishop said as he met with the archdeacon and dean of Daneford to plan Arthur and Sarah's funeral service and discuss the oversight of Daneford diocese until a new bishop was appointed.

Guy Morgan had met with Arthur and Sarah's children, Crispin and Diana, who had been happy to leave the liturgical details of the funeral to the clergy, but they had definite opinions on hymns and that one of them would give the appreciation.

The service having been sorted, the archbishop said, "Now, with regard to the diocese, the dean will be commissary, but I'm afraid that much of the day-to-day running of the diocese will fall on you, Archdeacon."

"That's no problem," replied Guy. "We'll liaise with Arthur's secretary, Louise Roberts, and look after things between us."

"The police said that Arthur failed to stop at a major junction," said the archbishop. "I wonder how he could have been so distracted?"

"Arthur was always a careful driver," replied Guy. "And he didn't appear stressed over Christmas. In fact, he was in super humour, quite chipper. He and Sarah were going to view some cottages they were interested in. They were thinking of buying a holiday home and were looking forward to a few days' break together."

"He was in great form when I saw him at the services in the cathedral," added the dean. "He was joking about how un-busy he was at Christmas compared to the rest of us!"

"Perhaps the post-mortem will throw some light on the causes," sighed the archbishop. "What a sad thing to happen, especially at Christmas."

The mobile phone on the table in front of them buzzed, and the archbishop looked at the screen. "It's the police. I'd better take this call, if you don't mind."

He moved off to one side of the room. Apart from a few 'I see's, the archbishop said little. But when he returned to his seat, his colleagues could see he was troubled.

"They've just done a post-mortem and toxicology test, and they found something which probably caused the accident. Arthur and Sarah had taken a good number of sleeping tablets. Now why would they take sleeping pills before setting off on a long car journey?"

"That doesn't make sense!" said Guy. "And anyway, I've never known Arthur to mention that either he or Sarah needed sleeping tablets. Though," he reflected, "that doesn't mean they didn't. I suppose he never did talk about private matters with me. Still, doesn't make sense."

"I agree," said the archbishop. "But that is what they found. I could never see Arthur or Sarah as users or abusers of drugs. There are further tests to be done, and the car, what's left of it, is also to be examined to see if there was any defect or anything like the brakes having been tampered with. I can only hope that the tabloids don't get hold of this information. You can imagine the field day they'd have! 'Pill Popper Bishop!'" He closed his eyes wearily. "The police also want to examine the See House, no doubt to see what is in the Easterbys' medicine chest. What a dreadful business this is all turning out to be!"

Chapter 40

Three months later

THE SUN WAS getting warmer and its light danced brightly on the tranquil sea as Lily watched a ferry leave Agoustini, the capital of the Greek island of Kefalonia. Tourists were beginning to appear, and she decided it was time she looked for a job at one of the island's many resorts. The wad of money her mother had left her, though considerable, wouldn't last forever, and she needed to start earning to pay for her accommodation. At the moment, she was staying in a basic hotel at cheap winter rates.

After making the picnic for the Easterbys, she had returned to her flat soon after the bishop and his wife had left. She'd then packed a suitcase and left on the overnight ferry to Liverpool. On arrival the next morning, she'd visited a travel agency and booked a flight to Kefalonia, where she easily found accommodation in Agoustini. In her flat and on the way to the ferry, her phone had kept ringing with calls from Louise. Not wanting anyone to know where she was, she'd dropped her phone overboard as soon as the ferry left port.

***

Meanwhile, back in Daneford, the police had found no sleeping tablets in the Easterbys' medicine chest and, checking with their GP, learned that no sleeping tablets had been prescribed. Yet in the remains of Arthur's car, they'd found a battered flask which still contained some coffee. Forensics had identified the presence of ground sleeping tablets in the coffee—quite a strong dose. It was so strong, in fact, they couldn't have fought off sleep.

Louise Roberts had become increasingly anxious about her friend Lily. Repeated phone calls got her nowhere: Lily's phone went dead, and when she visited Lily's flat she could see no one was in, yet Lily's car was still in the drive. In the end, she went to the police with her worries and accompanied them as they broke into the flat.

It was all neat and tidy, but it was evident from the staleness of the air that it had not been occupied for a few days.

The police searched the house for clues as to where Lily might have gone. They found her passport in her bedside table, so they limited their search to Ireland or England. Maybe she had used her driving licence as ID.

They also searched her mother's room. Louise explained that Lily's mother had had cancer and had recently passed away. That explained the presence of so much medication in the drawer beside the bed.

When the toxicology report came out about the presence of sleeping tablets in the Easterbys' blood and in their flask, one sharp policeman recalled seeing all the medication in the flat. Taking away all the tablets, they found a match for the tablets the Easterbys had taken.

The Easterbys' death became a murder investigation, and the search for Lily intensified, but no one had seen her or knew where she'd gone. A check on ferry and airport tickets also drew a blank. The police were baffled.

**

Daneford diocese was moving on. The funeral for the Easterbys had been huge and impressive. The archbishop had preached eloquently about Arthur's qualities and of a promising episcopal ministry cut short. Crispin Easterby had spoken movingly of dedicated and loving parents and of happy childhoods. A few weeks later, the family gathered at the See House to dispose of the contents and decide who was taking what as a keepsake and memento.

The diocesan episcopal electors had held one informal meeting to discuss possible candidates to succeed Arthur. The archdeacon and the dean had been asked to compile a profile of the diocese and its needs, to be discussed at their next meeting. Already there was some jockeying for prime position.

Anthony Parker had resigned from St. Aidan's immediately after Christmas and had, very quickly, secured the position of rector in a southern provincial town. He and Annabel were on an extended holiday in the sun, repairing and rekindling their relationship.

St. Aidan's parochial nominators were also meeting to discuss a possible successor. Harry White was strongly recommending that they consider Revd. Steve Adams in the next-door diocese.

***

Lily sat on the quayside soaking up the sun. She opened her bag and took out an envelope, which contained two items.

She re-read, for the umpteenth time, the letter her mother had left to be opened after her funeral.

Dearest Lily,

It has meant so much to me to have you as a daughter and also as a friend, and I love you dearly. Although you probably don't realise it, you have made my life worthwhile. It could have been otherwise.

I never really talked much about the past to you, and I have thought long and hard about whether to tell you what I am about to write. In one way, you would be better off not knowing, but in another way, I feel I owe it to you.

The fact is Bert MacDonald was not your father. You were born before I met Bert, and it is to his credit that when he married me he was more than happy to adopt you as his own and treat you as his daughter. He was much older than me, as you probably recall, and he died when you were six. I know that you have happy, if somewhat vague, memories of him.

Now I will tell you who your father actually is. This is very difficult for me as you now know him— Arthur Easterby.

We were going out together when he was a theological student, and we had talked about getting married. But when I became pregnant with you, he dumped me and disappeared out of my life. As you have probably found out working for him, he was always a bit of an arse.

Anyway, now I have told you, and I hope it does not come as too much of a shock. It may also explain why I would have nothing to do with the church.

You, Lily, have been everything to me. You gave me the purpose and strength to keep going when all I wanted was to curl up and die. I would have loved it so much if I had lived longer to share many more happy times together.

Your ever loving mum,
Rachel.

Tears still came to Lily's eyes when she read her mum's letter. Dabbing them away, she took out the other item in the envelope— her mother's passport. No wonder they had often been mistaken for sisters. The resemblance was uncanny.

"Rachel, Rachel! Is this where you are? I have been looking everywhere for you!"

Lily quickly put the items back into her bag as Alexandros, her Greek boyfriend, came up behind her and lovingly massaged her shoulders. She closed her eyes and began to relax.

About Ted Woods

I am a retired priest of the Church of Ireland, now living in Liverpool.

I served in a number of parishes in Ireland, North and South, most latterly in Rathfarnham, Dublin. I was a General Synod member, a Director of Ordinands, and worked in The Theological College looking after intern deacons in their final year.

For many years, I wrote a column on ministry for the Church of Ireland *Gazette*. For five years before retirement, I wrote a weekly 'soap' – 'Down in St. David's' – for the *Gazette* about the ups and downs of clerical life. On my retirement, another writer took over.

I have self-published a book on Kindle – *And Some There Were…* – a light look at 'the Good, the Bad and the Ugly' in the clergy of the Church of Ireland's past. The book includes twenty-five sketches, historically accurate, of priests and prelates from Reformation times to the twentieth century. With the aim of informing and entertaining, *And Some There Were…* features the rogues as well as the righteous, the murdered and the murdering, priests and bishops alike.

By the Author

And Some There Were:
Sketches of some Irish Anglican Prelates and Priests

Bishop

Beaten Track Publishing

For more titles from Beaten Track Publishing,
please visit our website:

Thanks for reading!

Lightning Source UK Ltd.
Milton Keynes UK
UKHW041207160222
398775UK00001B/31